SAVING GRACE

KIERRA WALKER

CONTENTS

Literary Freedom Publishing, LLC

909 W Main Street #154
Jacksonville, AR 72076

Visit our Website
www.literaryfreedompub.com

Printed in the United States of America.

First Printing: June 2021

Literary Freedom Publishing, LLC.

ACKNOWLEDGMENTS

I'd like to thank the ladies on Clubhouse for being my motivation to finish this book. The verbal encouragements, message, and invitations to participate in writing sprints aided greatly in my completion of Saving Grace. Whether you're a reader or writer, I thank you for getting me through this process! I look forward to many more late-night writing and talking sessions with you all.

PROLOGUE

ever, in a million years, would I have assumed I'd be in this predicament. Before now, my current circumstance would have seemed implausible, illusive almost. Now, I barely stand on my two feet, stuck inside this seemingly empty vessel I call a body, plagued with questions: Is this real? Is this really happening? Were we not mean to be? How do I move on and heal? What have I done to be deserving of such pain? How do I rid myself of the agony and start anew?

It's approximately 9:52pm and I find myself standing in the parking lot of Riverside Bar & Grill, the exact location where my husband and I reunited for the first time since our last day as seniors in high school; it had been 10 years but felt more like an eternity. With a hollow, short bottle of Green Apple Cîroc in hand, I drunkenly stagger across the vacant parking lot, in my overly worn black and white Chuck Taylors, of the now closed restaurant toward the river-bank. Though I've never proven to be a great swimmer, water has always brought a sense of tranquility over me. Perhaps it's due to my zodiac, Cancer, being a water sign, who knows.

With the empty bottle still in hand, I step foot into the foliage covering the riverbank's edge and bend into a squatting position, so that I may rest my bottom on solid ground. Feet pulled in near my buttocks and legs comfortably fixed against my chest, I rest my chin on my knees, eyes closed, allowing the sound of the water filtering downstream to carry my mind to an alternate reality. What I wouldn't give to choose another reality for myself right now. The pain that consumes me isn't something I'd wish on my worst enemy if I had one. I've never been one to throw a pity party but considering recent events I believe I have every right to wallow, to grieve.

My phone buzzes, breaking my serenity. I drop my legs and reach around to my left back pocket for my cell; my mother is calling for the eleventh time. I disregard the call, sliding the phone back into my pocket. As I reposition on the bank's edge, the liquor bottle I'd brought with me from the car and left at my side begins to tumble down the bank. My initial response kicks in, and I reach for the bottle. It evades my grasp and rolls even further down the bank, landing in the water, quickly being carried off by the current. Unexpectedly, the foliage underneath me gives, and like an avalanche the ground beneath me is practically nonexistent. Like a bowling pin, I descend downhill, gaining momentum as I approach the water's edge. As my right foot submerges into the murky waters, I scramble and manage to grab hold of a tree root. My heart is beating a mile a minute, scared I'm going to wind up in the river, knowing well floating is the closet that I've ever come to swimming. Besides, it's dark and I'm out here alone; this situation is quickly turning disastrous. I still myself, in an attempt to focus and propel myself back up the bank. I grip the root of the tree, allowing it to assume my full bodyweight, and it snaps. It freakin' snaps! Comparable to a tumbleweed, I fall back first into the river. In contrast to what I'd expect the bank and water meeting to be like, there's no ground, just water. Everything goes dark, and it's cold, bitterly cold, as I start to sink to the depths of a river that I've admired on my daily drive to work. Like a weighted anchor, my head submerges, leaving only my hand above surface. This is it, I'm gonna go, but would it be so bad? Is death the easy way out of my current feelings? Making up my mind, I relax and begin to take water into my nose and mouth. The feeling to resist drowning is strong, but maybe this is what God's intended for me. I close my eyes and succumb, slipping a bit deeper.

ONE

"Ma'am! Ma'am!" a muffled voice resounds, but I assume I could possibly be crossing over, going into the "light."

I can feel the water pushing me downstream, but, again, a voice speaks to me, "Ma'am, take my hand!"

Wait, that sounds like an actual person.

My body gains a surge of adrenaline and I break the surface, emerging, choking like crazy, incoherent of my surroundings.

"Yeah, that's it! I gotcha!" a deep, masculine voice greets my ears as I'm dragged back up the bank to solid ground. "Atta girl, come on, breathe."

I gasp for breath. Batting my eyes to regain my vision, I find a heavyset, middle aged Caucasian male wearing a red flannel shirt, coveralls, and steel toe boots staring down at me.

"Thank you..." escapes my lips and I sit in an upright position.

"Whoa, take it easy. You could have drowned, you know that?"

"I'm ok…"

"No, you're not. I'm calling 911," he insists, reaching for his cellular.

I blurt, "NO! Don't! I'm fine, really."

He pauses, giving off a confused dazed, "Ma'am, you could have died. You get that, right? If I hadn't been out here working tonight, you could have succumbed to the river's current and wound up on the riverbank miles down the way; you could have even been found. Please, let me do this, let me call help for you."

The look in his eyes in the moonlight speaks volumes. He's practically pleading with me, a complete stranger.

"Sir, thank you for pulling me out. You don't know just how appreciative I am, but there is no need to call anyone. I'm ok, I feel fine. I'm going to go home now."

He looks up, as if he's looking to God, and reluctantly replies in a sweet southern twang, "Young lady, don't make me regret not calling for help. I'd hate to hear that something actually happened to you and I could have helped prevent it."

"I promise, I'm going to my car and then home."

Against his original wishes, he walks me to my vehicle and waits for me to get in. I lock the doors and crack the driver's side window, "Remember, this place is closed now, so if you pull this stunt again no one will be here to help you. If I hadn't been working late to restore the deck on this building, you would have been at the mercy of the elements, the mercy of God. If you don't have a death wish, don't come alone again, or at all for that matter. And be careful." He taps the roof of my car and walks away.

I watch until he disappears behind the building from which he originally came.

I take an instant to absorb the events that have occurred, hunched over in the front seat of my car, clothes drenched to hell, and hair a kinky, matted mess. I rest my forehead on the steering wheel of my red, 2-door Honda Civic LX and blast the heat to take away the chill that's rapidly incapacitating my extremities. Meddling with the heat controls, my right hand grazes the radio volume and Monica's *Angel of Mine* seeps through my speakers.

When I first saw you, I already knew
There was something inside of you
Something I thought that I would never find
Angel of mine

Riverside Bar & Grill – May 2015 – 10 Year Riverside High School Class Reunion

"I don't believe I've ever seen you like this before, full of liquor. You were always so innocent back in school, you know, goody-two-shoes," Jessica, one of my best girlfriends and next-door neighbor during school, teases as we exit Riverside Bar & Grill from a night of celebration.

It's been ten years since we graduated high school. Where did the time go? At times it seems like only yesterday I was attending Friday night football games and picking out prom dresses. Life was so simple then.

"Yeah, well, everyone needs a little liquid courage to get through the night, right? Tonight's my night."

"It's all good. I'm just happy to see you're letting loose. It's rare to see this side of you..." Jessica rambles on as we meet up with the rest of the group.

"So, where we headed to next? You guys wanna go downtown? Oh, remember our favorite spot during out school days? Is it still open?" the most popular high school jock, Randy, suggests. After high school, we stayed connected. He opted for medical school, which is surprising considering his persona in high school.

He's speaking of Freddie D's, a hole-in-the-wall joint where the owner would allow us in, knowing we were all too young to enter, let alone drink. He didn't care, he only wanted our money.

"Ah, I think I'm going to call it a night. I'll catch up to you guys in the morning."

"Oh, don't be a party pooper! C'mon, I'll drive you," Randy pouts.

"Yeah, I don't know. I had a long day at work. I just want to sleep it off and start fresh tomorrow. I promise I'll be ready for the shenanigans tomorrow," I attempt to convince Randy and the rest of the group. They all start bickering amongst themselves, deciding the next move.

"You know, Grace is right. I drove in today and I'm a bit worn myself," a distant but once familiar voice communicates.

In an instant, I make a 180-degree turn, surprised to find my best friend standing before me.

Everyone mummers, concluding that Freddie D's is the next stop. I bid my farewell for the night, anxiously ready for my bed to envelop my body after a long day's work.

"Grace Middleton..." he speaks softly, lightly gracing my forearm with his fingertips.

I shyly face him head on, "Noah Richardson..."

"Where the hell have you been, girl?" I suddenly become victim of his embrace. I receive his hug, wrapping my arms around his back, taking a deep breath in, absorbing his subtly inviting cologne.

"I could ask you the same. It's been 10 years since I've seen you. Where are you now?"

"I'm still here, just in the most Northwestern portion of the state due to work. You?"

"Still here, working my life away," I chuckle nervously, careful not to reveal the fact that I can't stop staring. His bright, crystal brown eyes, intensely enriched melanated pigmentation, and strikingly present dimples are undeniably a sight for sore eyes.

"I see that, and might I add, you're more beautiful than ever Grace."

"Thanks. You're not too shabby yourself," I joke, struggling to contain my excitement. "I didn't see you here at all tonight until now. How is that? Where were you hiding out?"

"Not hiding out, just observing. You know me. You know how I do, or how we used to do at all the school dances while everyone danced the night away."

"Yeah, I remember. I just can't believe for the length of time we were all together tonight that I didn't run into you once," I give him a puzzled, suspicious look.

"Well, if I can be honest, I saw you earlier tonight and couldn't believe my eyes. I stared from afar, observing you. When I finally confirmed it was you, I didn't know how to approach you."

"What do you mean you didn't know how? We were practically best friends since kindergarten, joined at the hip since day one..."

"It's just..." he expresses apprehensively.

"Just what?" I stumble, nearly falling over nothing. Noah catches me.

"Whoa, easy. I believe someone's had too much to drink. How about I drive you home? You're welcome to phone me when you wake in the morning, I can get you back to your vehicle. I think it'll be fine parked here until then. What do you say?"

I widen my eyes, with hopes of making myself seem more alert, but the expression on Noah's face tells me otherwise. I secure my Honda and climb into Noah's Chevy Silverado, giving him the address to my apartment before we leave the parking lot.

The thirty-minute journey to my place serves as confirmation that we've missed much of one another's lives. We agreeably share details about our lives over the last 10 years. Noah shares that after high school, he relocated to the northern part of the state with his girlfriend, Carrie I believe was her name, for college and decided to settle; they married soon after but parted ways a few years later. After their divorce was final, he was offered a position with a major trucking company as an executive accountant, his dream job. He always had a knack for numbers. I went on to explain my position in today's finicky workforce and how unhappy I was with my progress. Contrary to the fact that I created a plan for myself long before high school ended, I accepted my current position to pay the bills, using my spare time to further develop my skills for my ultimate field of expertise. I unknowingly became complacent with my 9 to 5, waking up one day to find that I'd been there nearly four years and wasn't on track to accomplish anything. Fortunate for me, my mother's career-oriented drive helped coax me into my degree field, Business Administration with an emphasis in E-Commerce.

"This you?" Noah inquires, distracting me from our conversation. He pulls into my complex, parking in my assigned spot.

"Yep, this is me. Thank you for bringing me home," I grin, reaching for the door handle.

"Wait, let me get that for you," he scurries from the driver's seat to the passenger side, leaving his door open.

He takes my right hand in his, escorting me from his truck to the door of my apartment.

"Thank you for getting me home. I'm sorry I'm such a mess tonight, this isn't like me…" I fumble my words, but Noah interrupts.

"No trouble at all. I'm head over hills that I've been able to lay eyes on you after 10 years."

"Yeah, let's try not to be strangers. Would you like to come in for a bit?" I ask in a drunken stance, unlocking my door.

Noah slowly traces is tongue over lips, tapering off with a sensual, delicate bite at the end, "Everything in me wants to say yes, but I don't want my inebriated state determine my next move with you."

"Ok, Shakespeare, what is that supposed to mean?"

"It means…nevermind. I've already said too much. You have a great night, Grace. I'll see you tomorrow," he hands me a card with his number on it. With nothing further, he turns and walks away.

Is he walking away? Is he really walking away?

Unable to hold my tongue, "I can't believe you're just going to walk away from me. It's been 10 years. 10 YEARS! I never said anything because I assumed you and Carrie were happy, and I knew she was jealous of our friendship. But you're here now, finally, and you're just walking away?"

His steps cease. He turns and charges for me, walking faster than I've ever seen him move before.

His masculine hands take hold of either of my shoulders, shaking me a bit, *"Do you think I want to walk away from you? Huh? You think after 10 years that it's easy to tell you no, that I don't want to come into your place for a while longer?"*

"So, what's the problem then, Noah? Are you still with Carrie? If that's the issue, just so say" I throw my hands up in frustration.

He chuckles, *"You know damn well her name is Carmen, and, no, we aren't together. The problem is, after seeing you today I realized something that I knew long ago but never acted on it."*

"Acted on what?" I snap, growing tired of him speaking in code.

"You! Us! Grace, since the first time we shared that apple juice during recess in kindergarten I have loved you. There, I said it."

The words from his lips to my ears creates a ripple effect that echoes throughout my body, softly awakening my soul. I'm speechless. I'm unsure of what I expected him to say but it surely wasn't that.

"What?"

"You heard me. I love you; I've always loved you. Only now, I realize I kept you in the friend zone, keeping you close but not close enough, and I lost you to time. I won't do that again. Right here, right now, tonight, I'm admitting something that I've held on the tip of my tongue for years. I love you, Grace Middleton."

I leap into Noah's arms, gripping him forcefully. Little does he know, I've loved him for years, but I was always his best friend, and Carmen was always just...there.

"I love you, too." The words effortlessly roll off my tongue, like they belong there.

He breaks our embrace, looking down at me, *"Hey, you hear that?"*

I frown a bit, but my ears catch sound of what he speaks of. The opened door on his truck permits the sweet sound of Angel of Mine by Monica to filter through his speakers. We both smile, as the song brings back memories of our first dance together.

He was the first boy I shared a dance with the first boy to steal my heart.

The song fades and another takes its place. It's remarkable how one song can trigger a specific thought. I throw the car into drive, with home as my destination.

TWO

I wake to my alarm clock blaring. I slept through my usual 5am alarm, it's currently 6:12am. Feet to the floor, I walk hunchback to the bathroom, relieving myself, starting the shower. Undressed, I step into the shower, melting underneath the scolding hot water. Arms in a 90-degree angle and hands pressed against the wall directly underneath the showerhead, I surrender, granting the water total access to every inch of me, starting with my scalp. I close my eyes, imagining a time when I wasn't standing alone in the shower, when shower time was more pleasurable, memorable. Now, it's like a chore. It's cynically comical how life can alter our memories for the worse, making them bittersweet.

With no time to waste, I squirt a dollop of curl refining gel into the palm of my hands and finger comb from the roots to ends of my hair, producing a quick, shoulder length wash-n-go hairstyle for work. Patting myself dry and oiling down, I brush my teeth while searching relentlessly through my closet for something presentable to wear. I should have done this last night, but the fact is I'm not mentally, physically, nor emotionally prepared to return to work therefore I put off preparing.

Excusing my anxiety, I settle for a three-piece navy-blue pant suit and black t-strap heels, accenting the ensemble with a matching purse and jewelry. Grabbing my keys from the glass tray atop my dresser, I carefully trot across the mahogany wood floors to the foyer. Grabbing my genuine leather business bag, I set my alarm, heading for the driveway to my vehicle. Throwing my bags into the passenger seat, my body comfortably adapts to the black leather seats of my recently purchased Honda. Exhaling the last bit of anxiety from my lungs, I shift the car into reverse, backing into the street. Here I go, back to my normal routine.

Arriving at my place of employment earlier than expected, I park near the entrance, utilizing my badge for entry. One foot in front of the other, my eyes and mind are set on my destination; my office. I unlock the door and step inside, finding things the way I left them just a month ago. Before I can settle in, I hear a light tap at my door. I turn about to find my boss, Yvonne, standing in the doorway.

"Welcome back," she asserts firmly, planting either of her hands on her shapeless hips.

I nod, "Thank you, it's good to be back." She stares, which forces me to look around my office awkwardly in an effort to avert eye contact.

Shattering the silence, in walks my brilliantly flamboyant office neighbor, Shawna.

"Thank goodness, you're back! This place has gone to shit since you've been out..." she brushes past my boss, greeting me with an impromptu hug.

I jolt at her embrace, uneasily reciprocating the affection. As Shawna releases me from her grasp, staff members begin to pour into my office one by one, expressing their thoughts and prayers during my time of grief. Noticing that I've become overwhelmingly uncomfortable, Yvonne motions for everyone to exit, leaving me to reconcile in silence.

Unpacked, I turn my attention to the immaculate view I'm afforded from my seventh-floor office window into the heart of downtown. This was surely one of the incentives in accepting this position. Having not slept well the night before, I let out an extended yawn, distracting my attention from the window to a picture frame nestled on a console table in the far-left corner of my office. I swallow my pride, the pride deep inside that wants me to turn the other way, and tread leisurely to the picture frame, taking it into my grasp. Hands trembling, I lift the frame chest level, admiring the photo before me.

"Hey, Grace, we've got something..." Shawna interrupts, catching me off-guard, causing the photo frame to slip from my grasp. The frame descends, falling face first on the polished ceramic tile, leaving small broken fragments of glass and wood surrounding me.

Though I'm two seconds from a meltdown, I hold my composure.

"Hey, girl, what's up," I utter, holding back tears.

"Oh, no! Let me help with that!" she scrambles toward me, but I signal for her to stop.

"It's ok, I'll handle it. Everything ok?" I divert the conversation.

"Oh, no, I can come back. Are you sure you don't want me to help clean that mess up? I'm sure you wouldn't have dropped it if I hadn't walked in unannounced."

"No, really, it's fine. What do you have for me?" I insist, becoming somewhat irritated.

Realizing my rising frustration, Shawna responds, "Right, I'm sorry. Well, the team and I came together to get you a little welcome back gift." She gestures for a few others to enter.

"Surprise," a younger, lively coworker, Liana, squeals with excitement, holding an edible arrangement and a dozen white roses. "We wanted to get you something nice, and I remembered from a couple years back that you had something like this and absolutely loved it! So, I thought this would be the perfect gift! Besides, the edible arrangement you shared with us tasted *amazing*!"

Liana's right, I did enjoy the edible arrangement and dozen white roses, but it's the memory behind the gift itself that's left a bitter taste in my mouth.

March 2016

"Sorry to interrupt, but you have a delivery," Liana peeps into my office.

"A delivery?" I stand, a bit confused, as I'm not expecting anything.

"Yeah, a delivery! Delivery guy said it was for Grace Middleton and allowed me to sign for it down at the lobby," Liana strolls further into my office, placing a clear vase with a dozen white roses and an edible arrangement filled with my favorite fruits. "Oh, here's a card!"

Blushing, I take the envelope from Liana and open it. Nervously, I pull the card from the envelope and find a message:

Hello Beautiful
I do hope your day is going well.
Here's a little something to remember
me by. I hope you enjoy the strawberries
and pineapples.
- Noah.
My internal glow begins to radiate outward, as a smile reappears on
my face.

"You know I'm nosey. Who sent them?" Shawna peeks inside my office. I haven't been at this job long, but I've already found people who are solid. I'm extremely grateful for that because just last year I was struggling to find my footing in the workforce.

I turn to admire the roses and a sweet, familiar baritone voice greets my ears, "She knows who sent them..." Without hesitation, I make a 180-degree turn finding Noah standing in my wake.

"What are you doing here? I thought you were traveling today," I articulate, beaming from ear to ear.

"I am, but I had to stop by here to see you first. I had to see your beautiful face in person before hopping on that plane to Chicago." Noah approaches, towering over me.

Whether he's aware or not, it's the small genuine gestures that make me the happiest. Somehow, he continuously manages to amaze me with his sincerity and generosity.

"Thank you, Noah. This is beautiful and completely unexpected." *I blush, unable to maintain eye contact.*

"Anything for you. You know that. Say, I'd better run. If I miss my flight, I'll be pressed to drive for hours to get to Chicago in time for this conference."

"Understood. Yes, you should go," *I gesture with my right hand. Honestly, I loathe the fact that he'll be away. It feels as if I'm missing a portion of myself when he's not around.*

He takes his hand to my chin, elevating it just enough for eye contact to be made. "You're my favorite girl, you know that right?" *I nod.* "Good. I want you to remember that. Mark my words."

"What does that mean?" *I inquire. My eyebrows peek, as does my curiosity.*

"Just remember those words, my love. I gotta run. I'll text you when I land," *he leaves me with a kiss on the forehead.*

No sooner than he disappears, my snooping coworkers crowd my office, speaking on Noah's romantic efforts.

"Girl, where the heck did you meet this one? He's delivering gifts to the job and everything. I've never had anyone do that." *Shawna pouts.*

"I wouldn't buy your crazy tail anything either. You beat your men," *Liana comments, clearing her throat. We all chuckle at Liana's statement because it's true. Shawna has the worst luck with men.*

To smooth things over, "When the time presents itself, Mr. Right will come along. You just need to be ready," *I reassure her.*

"Aw, thank you Grace. At least someone in here has something positive to say about my love life," *she teases.*

I could listen to the two of them joke back and forth all day, but Noah's gifts have my undivided attention.

"The bouquet and edible arrangements are absolutely beautiful," Yvonne compliments, changing the subject, distracting me from my wandering thoughts.

"Thank you. They're both my favorite."

"He seems to know you well," Yvonne suggests.

"Yeah, he does. Jokingly, I tell him quite often that he knows me better than I know myself." I smile.

"Grace? Are you ok?" Liana calls to me, pulling me from the daydream triggered.

Returning to consciousness, "Yes, I'm fine let me get this cleaned up." Thought I attempt to hold them back, tears begin to flow freely onto my cheeks.

"Was it something I did or said? Is it the gift? Do you not like it?" Liana questions in a panic.

"No, no. It's not the gift. This is a beautiful gift, really, and I'm appreciative of you guys for making my first day back memorable. Things are just tough right now."

"Right, of course. Duh. Well let me help you get this glass up," she squats before me, picking up the larger pieces.

"Oh, you don't have to do that. I'll get it."

"No, I insist," she rebuts.

"Liana," I snap. "Please, allow me. I can handle it." Timidly, she rises and shyly backs away, exiting the room. Without speaking, Shawna and the others retreat quietly, closing the door behind them.

Ignoring the broken picture frame, I trot to my chair. A nervous wreck, I find myself shuddering and quivering to keep my squalling at a bare minimum. The last thing I need is for my coworkers to consider me broken, catering to me because of recent events. I don't want special treatment or sympathy. I'm beyond ready to get back into the swing of things without having an emotional breakdown each time Noah comes to mind.

With my first day in the books, I return home and change into something more comfortable, settling onto my oversized sectional with a tall glass of red wine. No thought in mind, I aimlessly thumb through the television channels hoping something catches my eye.

Tap Tap

An unexpected knock at my door breaks my channel surfing. I tiptoe across the cool wood floors to the door.

"Surprise!" my mother sounds, inviting herself in. She waltzes in, leaving my father standing on the other side of the door.

He chuckles, rolling his eyes, "Hi, sweetheart." I reciprocate his hug, gesturing his entry.

I lock the door behind me and trail my parents into the kitchen. They've brought over my favorite meal and wine.

"Thank you for bringing this by. I'm starving but didn't want to cook."

"I figured you would be and I know what you love, so your father and I thought we'd surprise you. How was work today?"

22

Mom questions me, pulling a plate from the cabinet to warm my dinner. I knew the questions were coming. She can't control herself.

Against my original thought, I share my day with my parents, explaining how the edible arrangement and bouquet of white roses gifted to me by my coworkers triggered me, that I didn't feel as if I was ready to return to work.

"So, you think you need more time off dear? That very well could be true. You take as long as you need. Losing a spouse isn't easy. You've only been off for a month; you may need longer. Things like this take time," my father weighs in.

My mother places my plate before me and takes a seat at the dining table with Dad and I.

"Personally, I feel like now is the time to push through. You're in the height of your career after many years of wandering meaninglessly through the workforce. You know I was much younger than you when I lost my mother and I had to raise your aunts and uncles while your grandfather worked to provide for us. If I can do that at 13, you can do it at your age. You're grown, you can handle this. You've gotta dig deep and persevere," Mom declares.

"Darlene, honey, you must understand what Grace is going through right now. She lost her husband. She needs time to heal, time to grieve."

"Charles, when I lost my mother there was no time to grieve or feel. I had to raise my siblings. Going through that has made me the strong, resilient woman I am today."

"So, because I have feelings and emotions behind the death of my husband that makes me weak?" I drop my fork onto the plate, interested to see what she'll say next.

"All I'm saying is, you need to put your big girl panties on and get back out in society. Locking yourself in this house, staying home from work, isn't helping you heal. What will help you heal is getting back to work, interacting with people, and so on."

Mom's comment sends her and Dad into an argument that I don't want to bear witness to. After several minutes of sitting between their disagreement, "Ok, that's enough. Could you please go? I'm tired and should get in bed soon."

"But it's early…" Mom states with a confused expression.

"Darlene, you heard her. Get your purse, let's go."

With an attitude, Mom grabs her purse and sashays toward the front door. She exits, not saying goodbye. Dad turns to me, issuing an apology.

"It's ok. I love you, daddy."

"I love you, too, pumpkin. I'll check on you later." I nod, closing and locking the door before Dad approaches the car.

Disappointed with how my mother acted, I clear the dining table and head for bed, snuggling under my weight of my comforter with my phone in hand.

"Hey girl," I answer a Facetime call from my bestfriend Naomi.

As my parents did, Naomi asks about my first day back at work and how I'm feeling. In contrast to how I feel about revealing my feelings and emotions to my mother, I feel utterly comfortable speaking with Naomi. She gives the best advice, especially now.

"It sounds like you need more time off, Grace. You just lost her husband; this can't be easy. Not everyone is able to cope within the same timeframe. You may need more time off. Know that there's nothing wrong with that, there's nothing wrong with the way you're feeling right now. Have you considered going back to the therapist I recommended?"

"Yeah, I've considered it but it seems that all I do is cry while I'm there. I don't know if it's actually helping."

"Goodness, girl. You sound like my clients. Crying is part of the healing process. You're paying that therapist, cry all you want to. And if you're crying then that means their doing something right. Besides, I wouldn't have recommended you to her if I had thought she wasn't one of the best in our field. I sent you to one of the best. Use your sessions to your advantage. You know what, here's an idea. Why don't you take FMLA? I'll give Shandra a call for you and see if she can doctor up something for you to give HR. I'm sure she can have you something first thing in the morning."

"You always know what to do when I'm feeling lost."

"You're not lost, you're simply finding yourself," Naomi states, calming my spirit. "Say, why don't you use the time off and go visit that cabin your parents have off the lake."

"You know what, you might be on to something."

We continue for another hour, praying, laughing, and crying together before ending the call.

I wake to an email from Shandra with the information I need to provide to HR to request more time off. Skipping breakfast, I forward the email over to Yvonne and she agrees to handle everything on my behalf.

With work squared away, I decide to take Naomi's advice.

Starting in the kitchen, I pack perishable and non-perishable items to take with me to the cabin, followed by packing two large suitcases full of clothing and personal items I know I'll need while away.

With the car loaded, I buckle my seatbelt and adjust my rearview mirror, destination set for the lake house.

THREE

I start one of my many classic playlists, including artists like Brandy, Tyrese, Joe, Faith Evans, SWV, and Xscape to help soothe me. Out on the open road, my mind wanders as the music sifts through the speakers. My mind begins to wander to the only thing that's brought me reprieve over the years: Noah. It seems as though each time I try to tuck the hurt away, it all regurgitates, causing me gut-wrenching pain. The ride to the lake house isn't long, but my traveling there doesn't seem to be passing fast enough for my liking. My mind is progressively becoming overwhelmed with thoughts of *him* and how much different life would be if he were still here. I'm exhausted with the weeping, the melancholy.

"Make a right turn in a half mile," the navigation voices, awaking me from my thoughts. Wiping the tears from my eyes, I decrease my speed and make a right turn off the highway onto the gravel road. I smile, as the sound of the rocks popping underneath the tires and carriage of the car brings back memories of my childhood spent here during summer and spring break. As a teenager, I hated coming here. It was always so secluded. I couldn't contact my friends and we only have an antenna for television, so I spent most of my time here reading on the deck looking out over the water. I eventually found peace with our visits to the lake house but have yet to return since my senior year in high school. Showing up here today is different though, it's not like I remembered it at all. I'm feeling a strong sense of nostalgia, like I'm returning home. The road to the lake house is long and winding, as the property sits over a mile off the highway. Approaching the house, I roll down the driver side window and take in the aroma of the wildly grown grass, pollenated trees, and fresh morning rain. The since of sadness seems to be melting away from my body, giving my feelings and emotions some relief, even if it's temporarily.

Coming to a rolling stop, I shift the car into park and climb out. In two trips, I take the groceries and suitcases to the porch, leaving everything by the front door while I take a moment to absorb my surroundings. The first thing I notice is my parents haven't been here in quite some time. The high grass and cobwebs accenting the posts on the porch is proof of that. I retrieve the door key from the place my mother's hidden it for years, and let myself in. The house seems dirty, but the bones of the house are still good. I walk around, exploring my surroundings. Everything is just as I remember.

Before I can put anything away, it's apparent the place needs some dusting and polishing. I quickly check to ensure the electricity and water are working properly and proceed to clean, starting with the kitchen and dining areas. Figuring it'll be easier to clean if I'm in a groove, I run for the record player in the den. There were plenty nights that I would watch my parents pull out their wine, fresh fruits, cheeses, and so on, pull one of their favorite albums out, and place it on the record player. Once the needle was set to the record, the music began. There's nothing different about today. Next to the record player are several old milk crates filled with vinyl records. Thumbing through the records, my fingers land on Parliament's P-Funk. It's just the song I need to get my cleaning underway.

After an hour of vigorous cleaning, I put everything way, turn the music off, and realize I'm too exhausted to cook. I work to put away the food I brought with me and settle for a sandwich. It doesn't take long to consume the club sandwich and chips. I secure all the doors and turn all lights out expect for the light above the oven and the floor lamp in the far corner of the living room. I head right for my bedroom, throwing a suitcase onto the bed so that I can unpack. As I place my clothing into the dresser adjacent to the bed. Pictures adorning the wall catch my attention, distracting me from my process. The walls are coated with pictures of Naomi and myself, my parents, the surrounding neighbors, and celebrations we all shared. This trip is definitely what I needed to bring some mental and emotional release from Noah's death and the world. Although I probably need to, I opt out of showering and slip into a set of oversized shorts and a tee. Before I know it, sleep consumes me.

The nostalgic feeling I went to bed with has fled me. I wake feeling like utter shit. Today, I feel like utter shit. Still in bed, my attempts to get up have failed because of the abdominal pain that's disabled my movement. I clench at my tummy as my muscles feel like they're being wringed like a wet bath towel. As I contemplate moving once more, nausea comes over me a little too quickly. I throw my comforter back and sprint to the bathroom. Barely making it, I land my head right over the commode and vomit spills from my mouth violently. After three rounds of losing what little contents I have in my stomach, I overhear my phone ringing. Panting, I use the back of my right hand to wipe away the slime from my mouth before heading for my phone.

It's Naomi. I forgot to call her when I made it. With one motion, I hit the answer button and speak first.

"Hey! What's up?" I ask avoidantly, hoping I'm not letting on to the fact something is wrong.

"What's up with me? I was just checking to make sure you made it ok. Are you alright? I didn't hear from you yesterday."

No matter how hard I try, Naomi knew me better than I could ever hide. I try time and time again to not let onto the fact that something is off, but she knows me better than anyone. I can hear it in her voice and I know eventually she'll ask.

"I made it in ok and went to bed feeling fine, then this morning I woke up not really feeling well. I threw up a few times. I guess I'll have to go out and get me a few things because I definitely didn't pack anything to aid me in sickness outside of headache medicine."

"Don't move. I can bring you a few things. Just rest until I get there. You're probably dehydrated and your stomach is upside down. Give me about an hour, and I'll be there."

"No, I can't ask you to do that—"

"You didn't ask. It's my suggestion. See you soon. Relax until I get there, ok?"

"Alright. You're a lifesaver. I am a little dehydrated, and my throat is kind of sore."

"See, I knew it. Alright, I'm on my way to the store and then I'll be on my way to you."

"Naomi, thank you," I let out a sigh of relief. Truth is, I'm in no shape to drive anywhere at the moment. Her offer is right on time.

"Of course."

I disconnect the call and return to the bathroom. The smell of vomit is fresh and I can't take it any longer. I adjust the shower to the right temperature, strip, and step inside. The water seems to bring some life back but I'm still feeling feeble.

By the time I'm done freshening up, I hear a car door closing and footsteps approaching over the gravel. I slip into a robe and meet her at the door.

"Naomi!" I sing, opening my arms to greet her. She reciprocates, holding me tightly, stroking the center of my back with her freshly manicured hands.

Breaking out embrace, "What do we have here?" I take the attention from myself and to the two plastic bags she's brought with her.

"Good question," she makes her way to the couch. I sit next to her. "Alright, I brought Sprite and Ginger Ale. I know sometimes one or the other works. I got you some crackers, Ritz, since I know those are your favorite. Let's see," she pauses, continuing to comb through the bag. I lean forward, curious to see what other treats she has. I find that she's brought juice and bottled water with her as well.

"How are you feeling now?"

I place my hand on Naomi's. I know she isn't just asking me about the nausea.

"I'm ok, for once. Really. Last night was a huge success. Just getting away and doing a little cleaning occupied my mind a bit. I was so tired afterward, I just laid down, and before I knew it, I was out. I haven't rested that well in weeks."

"Oh, that's great, Grace. I know you haven't slept well in a while, so I'm glad. I don't want to interrupt your time. I just wanted to bring you—"

"Interrupt my time? Please, girl. I could use your company if you're up to it."

"Me? Up to it? Of course! Anything in particular you want to do? Movies? Baking?"

"Uh, I don't know. I was thinking about getting out on the property today, getting some fresh air."

"Yeah, I noticed the grass and curb appeal could use some work. When's the last time you got out in the garden? That might be good for you, shoot for the both of us. Maybe afterward we can cook? I don't mind running to the store."

"That's perfect. I can't tell you the last time I got my hands dirty. And I think we have everything we might need to cook. I brought plenty of food from home. Stay here with me. It'll be fun!"

Naomi smiles, which makes me smile. Her suggestion of gardening makes me laugh. It's been ages since I got in the dirt and planted something new, but even thinking about doing so brings me some excitement.

"I didn't bring any clothes. Do you have any you can lend me?" Naomi and I are around the same size, so her borrowing clothes isn't a problem.

"Duh! Follow me. I need to change into something more appropriate myself."

I lead Naomi to my bedroom and hand her something more comfortable to move around in.

"Before we go out, have you a few sips of Ginger Ale and a couple crackers. You'll want something on your stomach before doing yardwork."

"Yes, mother!" I tease her. She's always been the mother between us two. She's a natural leader.

I change clothes and head right for the kitchen, waiting for Naomi to join me.

"Ready?"

I nod.

Our first stop is the shed outback. It takes some elbow grease to open the door, but once we're inside we find we have everything we need to get started.

"Ok, you get the gardening scissors, and I'll get some dirt. Ooh, there are still pots that are unused. We can use them. Oh, this is so exciting!" I practically jump around at the idea. I've always had a green thumb. I can't wait to get my fingers into the soil. Something about growing and sustaining life is beautiful to me.

"You got it, captain!" Naomi says, aligning the fingertips of her right hand to her eyebrow. Giving me a cute salute, she grabs her items and exits the shed.

I lay eyes on an old school lawn mower. It's one of those that don't have a mow. It's perfect! With my hands full, I drag it out along with the other things I'd already picked up and make my way to Naomi.

"Ok, you go over there and start cutting what's dead."

"Why? I wanna plant something too. You know, get my hands dirty. That whole...thing." Naomi laughs, and I can't prevent the laughter that comes from me as well.

"Oh please. We both know you don't have the gift hun. That's why you're going to cut the dead stuff, and I'm going to tend to the plants that are here already right after I'm done mowing."

"Yeah, ok!" she agrees, unashamed of the fact that gardening just isn't her cup of tea.

She gets to work and so do I. I check on her ever now and again. As I cut the grass, I can only think of how great a friend she is, always at my aid when I need her most.

It takes the greater part of the morning for us to get the yard in order, but after stepping back to admire our work I realize we've done a damn good job. The house and landscape look just as it did when Dad would work his magic. We both pull our phones out, recording our victory.

"Whew! I don't think I've worked this hard since we played sports in school! C'mon, let's get out of this sun and get cleaned up."

"Say less. I'm surely ready to relax now."

We enter the house, being met by coolness. Grabbing a bottle of water, we both go our separate ways to shower and meet back in the kitchen.

"You bathed fast!"

"No, ma'am, you just take long showers," I laugh. She's always been that way.

"Ha! You're right, I'll give you that one. So, what did you decide to cook?"

"I think I'm going to make us something light, like chicken pot pie or chicken noodle soup. What do you think?"

"Oh, yes! You make the best chicken noodle soup! I'd love some. That'll go perfectly with those Ritz crackers I brought along this morning."

"Alright, chicken noodle soup it is."

I immediately go to work, mixing and matching ingredients to make a meal we'll both be satisfied with. As I work, she turns on some 90s R&B. I glide around the kitchen with ease, letting the rhythm of the music take me away. Looking in the cabinet for one final ingredient, I come across a pink colored bag. It's a giant bag of sugar, seated right next to a small tube of multicolored sprinkles. The grand idea of making cupcakes crosses my mind. I drag out the necessary ingredients for the cupcakes, along with bowls and other mixing tools that I'll need. Depending on how my tummy feels after dinner, I'll indulge in a cupcake. Hopefully, whatever sickness I was feeling earlier will be gone so that I can enjoy my treat in peace.

As I begin mixing the cupcake batter, I fond memory surfaces.

May 2017

"So, you're really gonna make cupcakes that look like those in that magazine?"

"I sure am. Are you doubting my skills, sir?" I give him the side eye.

"Absolutely not. I trust you. Do ya thang baby," he vocalizes, placing his hands on my hips from behind. He comfortably adjusts his middle section against my behind and leans in, planting a tender kiss on my left cheek. I lean into him, eventually turning to face him. Words aren't needed between us. We always seem to communicate telepathically, using only our eyes and pure energy between us to speak.

We've been seeing one another for nearly a year now but each time I'm with him it seems like we're back at Riverside Bar and Grill all over again. I become bashful, shy in his presence. To maintain my composure, to keep from melting, I look away, redirecting my attention on something less intense.

Pulling away from his embrace, "You'd be trusting right. I know my way around cupcake making. You'd be surprised."

I open the oven to check the cupcakes, and the sweet aroma escapes, filling the room. I've been making cupcakes for years but this is the first time I've cooked a dessert for us to enjoy intimately. I want them to be something he'll remember.

The timer on the countertop goes off just in time. Grabbing an oven mitt, I remove the cupcakes and place them on the stovetop. Turning to finish prepping my homemade icing, I see that Noah's already volunteered himself as a taste tester.

"So, how'd I do?

"Baby, this icing is amazing! You did the damn thang! If the icing tastes like this, I can only imagine what the cupcakes will be like!"

I'm happy with his report. He's such a foodie, so his opinion defi-nitely has weight behind it.

"I'd be a liar to say it isn't delicious, Grace. But, you know, I'm more interested in finding out how you taste."

Damn near choking, "What?" I fumble over my words.

"Oh, nothing..." he replies sarcastically, stepping away from the icing. He may be moving but he doesn't take his eyes off me.

"No, you said something. What did you say? Repeat it, please."

My eyes follow his tall, richly melanated muscular physique as he creeps toward me mysteriously. Looming over me, he repeats himself and I'm floored. In the last year that we've been reconnected, he hasn't once said anything like this. Now, sure we've had some intimate encounters but none have resulted in sex. One of the first things he told me after we found one another again following the high school reunion was that he wouldn't rush things, that he wanted to get to know the woman I'd grown into during the years we were apart.

As he leans in, my heartrate increases. Noah and I have been so caught up in our feelings and in the way we make each other happy, sex hasn't been brought to the table yet. We are more than sexually attracted to one another. We always have been, but reconnecting has been our number one priority.

"Have some?" Noah lifts his right index finger. There's pink icing covering his fingertips.

"What are you doing? Here, give me your hand," I reach for a dishrag to wipe his hand but he stops me.

Before I can speak, Noah uses his index finger to smudge icing on the tip of my nose. He leans in a bit closer, kissing the tip of my nose, decorating his lips with icing.

Though he licks his lips to get the icing off, there's still some lingering about the corners of his mouth. As the tension builds

37

between us, I feel compelled to lick it off. Acting before my thoughts align, my tongue snakes across his lips, devouring the leftover icing.

"Mmmm..." a deep moan escapes his full lips.

"Oh, you like that?" I tease him innocently, reaching behind his back to grab the bowl of icing.

Extending my hands upward, I unbutton his baby blue dress shirt with one hand, and with the other, leave a nickel size dollop of icing where the buttons once covered his chest.

"I hope you're prepared to lick that off." His voice is playful, his eyebrows perfectly arched with wonder.

I give him a smirk, ready to take our relationship to the next level. I'm barely able to put the icing down before the tension between us erupts. For a moment, we are intimate, gentle with one another, as Noah uses the back of his hand to caress the right side of my face. Starting at my temple, his fingertips glide effortlessly past my eyebrow and over my cheekbones to the base of my neck. Pausing, the once kind and gentle nature Noah possessed quickly turns into a heatwave of emotions between the two of us. His enormous hands firmly cuff the base of my neck, taking my breath, as he gazes into my eyes without blinking once. A fire within me that has long laid dormant is reigniting. My first reaction is to control it, but the tingling sensations pulsating through my body take control. With my sexual senses, emotions, and feelings at an all-time high, I release a ragged breath as I take Noah into my embrace. Triggering his senses, Noah cuffs my apple bottom into the palm of his hands, lifting me up, firmly centering me on the kitchen sink.

A yelp escapes my mouth as I feel myself slipping into left side of the sink.

"I won't drop you unless it's to drop you onto me. Relax and trust me. Let me take care of you." I do trust him, with everything in me.

Instantaneously, Noah and I go at it, unable to pacify the intensity between us. He strips my clothes from my body, one piece at a time, starting with my shirt first. It comes off so quickly, I forget I even had one on. He tugs at my pants. I use my hands to lift my body up to come out of each leg, with Noah's help.

I'm exposed, my body his for the taking.

"You're beautiful, Grace." His eyes are saying things his mouth won't. He resituates my body to the countertop to the left of the sink. They're more space on the left side.

Eyes locked on me, his hands slither up my thighs toward my pelvic region. Smoothly, he dips his fingertips into the icing, drawing my attention away from him.

"Lie down," he grumbles, his voice authoritative in nature. I recline my position, my back across the cold counter. The coolness feels good since my flesh feels like it's on fire. Starting with my ankles, Noah drizzles icing over me, curving it in a s-pattern. As the drizzle decorates me, my body begins to shudder from the sensation and my sexual energy elevates.

When I see Noah's neck crane toward my inner thigh, I brace myself, knowing that if his kisses down low are anything like his kisses on my mouth, I'm in trouble.

"You smell delicious, but this icing has nothing on you..."

His sentence is finished with his tongue trickling over the icing on both my thighs. I wiggle in delight, in utter pleasure. It isn't until I feel the tip of his tongue flick over my pearl that I realize the icing is gone and I'm about to be devoured better than any cupcake could ever be. Swiftly removing my lace panties, Noah wastes no time slathering my juices over his face.

"Noah," I whisper.

I'm seconds from exploding. My hips rotate to the rhythm of his tongue as he continues to pleasure me relentlessly. There's no holding back, he's giving me everything he's got and it feels amazing. A slight movement on his part causes me to look over at him. I notice one of his hands disappear from my sight. Using my peripheral vision, I get a glance at his manhood. It's practically draping over his hand as he caresses it to a stiffened state. As he presumes to pleasure me, he strokes himself, eventually bringing both of us to an orgasm so powerful I nearly fall off the sink.

"I told you, I won't let you fall," he says commandingly, taking my now limp body into his arms. Taking me to the dining table, we kiss once more, this time more passionately as I taste the sweetness that's erupted from my body just moments before. He gently plants my body on the surface of the rustic wood table and fiddles with his pants, completely removing them and his boxers.

In a frenzy, our hands wrestle for dominance over one another. Lying me on my back, he pulls me to the edge of the dining table, my ass cheeks hanging ever so slightly over the edge. I take a deep breath and close my eyes, preparing myself for his entry. His entry into my moistened canal triggers me much more than I anticipate and I cream instantly, making it easier for him to invade me. He sets the tone and I follow suit, gripping his arms at the elbow, crying out in ecstasy from his deep strokes, elongated shaft, and girth. I close my eyes and succumb to the ride. The wait to have Noah in such an intimate manner is well worth the wait.

After an intense love-making session, we find ourselves nestled on the oversized sofa in the living room.

"You know, I really like this place, but have you thought anymore about buying it? We'd need a larger house eventually, you know, as time goes on and things in our lives expand."

My brow raises and I sit up, "Expand? What do you mean?" I'm curious to what his response will be.

"I mean, I want us to live together, grow together. I want to marry you, have kids with you," Noah announces unexpectedly, staking his claim in my life permanently. I can't say I'm surprised, hell I want the same thing, I just wasn't expecting him to admit it so willingly.

"Children, as in plural?" I ask, just to clarify.

"Of course. Two boys, one girl. A junior for me, a little girl with her middle name as Grace."

"I see you have it all thought out. I love it and share your same vision. I just want to ensure w can afford kids and other things without struggling. You know, I'm just getting into my career and you're already set. I just want to ensure—"

"Hey, you're thinking too far into it. We've got all the time to do that, as long as we're together. I'll take care of things until you find something you're passionate about, ok? No need to worry."

If I didn't already know before, I know now. I'm undeniably, unashamedly, and passionately in love with Noah. Our future is more than promising, it will be perfect.

"Earth to Grace! Did you hear me? I said thanks for the soup." I turn to look at Naomi, who's now sitting at the kitchen table with a soup spoon in her hand.

"I...I heard you," I stutter, snapping out of my flashback to my first intimate session with Noah. In the exact place that Naomi sits is where he brought me complete and immeasurable pleasure. "You're welcome. I made it for the both of us. After a long day of yardwork, I figured we could use a light meal."

"Definitely. Gardening, though you gave me the crappy part, was a lot of fun. Listen," Naomi pauses to take a sip of her soup. "I wanted to invite you to my housewarming party. I wanted to wait until I got the go ahead, but I'm moving in as soon as I get back to the city and I can't completely settle in if you don't come and celebrate with me."

A forced reassuring smile appears on my face. I'm not sure if I'm ready to be around other people who I might not know, or worse, those who I do who want to ask me over and over how I'm doing. At the same time, I don't want to leave my friend out to dry, especially when she's been nothing but supportive.

"I'll be there. I'm so happy for you. You didn't tell me you closed on the house."

"Well, I was waiting til' it was official."

We converse more about the closing of her new home, need for new furniture, and so much more. We end the night by indulging in the decadent cupcakes I decided to whip up last minute.

"Listen, today has been amazing. I'm going to go ahead and get back home so that I can get things together. I'm beyond excited and grateful that you've agreed to come. I love you, girl, and I'm proud of you."

Naomi rises from the table and wraps her arms around me in a loving embrace. Only this time if feels different. It doesn't feel like it normally does, or has in the last few weeks, while I've been grieving. Right now, it feels like it should, a normal hug from my friend and for that I'm appreciative.

FOUR

*E*xactly four weeks have passed, and tonight is Naomi's housewarming party. I haven't seen her house yet. She's refused to send me any pictures in advance. She's determined to ensure I show my face.

In preparation of the party, I opt for a long, hot, relaxing bubble bath. I figure this may be a good way to ensure my nerves are settled before getting out on the open road. As usual, I decide on a wash-n-go style. I've never been much of a hairstylist, so a little water, leave-in-condition, and a little finger combing always does the trick when I'm in a squeeze.

I sit down at my vanity and examine myself. My jawline seems sharper, considering my face has always been round, and I have dark circles under my eyes. I've aged or at least it feels like I have. Pulling out my makeup and necessary utensils, I start with my eyes, lightly applying concealer underneath my eye to hide the sleepless nights and emotional turmoil I find myself in often as of late. Blending it in, I then apply a base coat of foundation and a few other fixings to highlight certain facial features then work to get my hair in order. Using my spray bottle to apply some additional water to my hair before detangling, I begin at ends of my hair, carefully including my way upward toward the root by sifting my fingertips through my hair. As I run my fingers through, my middle finger becomes entangled. I withdraw my hand and opt for a wide tooth comb instead. Using the same method, I start at the ends and work my way up toward the root. My anxiety begins to rise as I realize that I've totally neglected my hair. I'm literally losing hair in knots and strands as I work to detangle. It's a complete mess.

Frustrated, I let out a deep sigh. The first thing I want to do is message Naomi and let her know I won't be able to make it. As much as I want to be in the mood tonight, happiness seems to be eluding me.

"No, not tonight. I'm not going to flip out," I talk myself down.

I can't allow this ruin my evening. I'm determined to enjoy myself tonight. Considering I recently lost my spouse, I allowed to have a few breakdowns here and there.

Checking my hair and makeup once more, fluffing my dampened curls to make my hair appear fuller. I move to the bedroom, dressing in a casual fit I bought some months back. I'm surprised to find that it doesn't fit as snug as it did when I first purchased it. I actually have some wiggle room.

Only a few minutes late, I arrive at Naomi's in one piece. I'm shocked I haven't heard from her before enow. Either she's just getting started or too occupied by guests to realize I haven't arrived yet. I retrieve Naomi's housewarming gift from the backseat and make my way to the main entrance. I ring the doorbell and wait to be greeted.

"Grace!" Naomi greets me cheerfully.

She's dressed in a champagne bodycon that perfectly accentuates her curves. Her hair is in a messy bun, and might I add that she's glowing from the inside out. This is probably the happiest I've seen her.

"Naomi! Congratulations! Your home is drop dead gorgeous! Here, I got you something." I enter the foyer of her home, reciprocating her warm, welcoming embrace.

"Oh, you didn't have to!"

"Girl, please! Of course, I did. Come on, give me the grand tour ma'am. I can't wait to see the whole house!"

"Well follow me, come on." Naomi takes my hand in hers and like two little girls, we bounce with excitement from room to room. We tour the entire house, minus her bedroom, and on our way back into the common area, we run into some friends of Naomi.

"Everyone, this is Grace, my best friend. Grace, this is Edward, we used to work together. This over here is Pearl. She works in HR."

Everyone shakes my hand as we make our way through the crowd. The guests are inviting and polite, total contrast to me returning to work. It was stuffy and uncomfortable. I felt smothered and alone simultaneously. So, being here tonight is the change of pace I needed to get back in the groove.

Pulling me from the crowd, "Why don't you grab a glass of champagne and come see the master bedroom. Everyone else has seen it, but I can give you an exclusive private tour!" she squeals, beaming with excitement.

"I'll take some water and a few crackers. I don't really have much of an appetite tonight."

"Yeah, I see you're slimming down. You look good. Are you feeling ok?"

"Yeah, I'm good. Still taking things one day at a time. You know, your home is absolutely gorgeous. I'm beyond proud of you. This is a great achievement. You're my role model."

"Hmm, I like how you changed the subject there, but thank you. I'm looking forward to us having some great times here."

My eyes drop, unable to look into hers. She called me out on changing the subject. I'm not up for telling people how I truly feel at the moment. I just find it easier to talk about something else.

Making it inside, Naomi's bedroom is the stuff of dreams. It's grand and elegant, just like her personality. As we move further into the bedroom, her walk-in closets are to die for and is perfect for her extensive wardrobe.

"Over here. Come on." She pulls me to the bathroom, which is even more exquisite than the damn bedroom. She's really got it going on.

We're interrupted by one of the guests looking for the restroom.

"It's on the other end of the hall to the left. You can't miss it," she redirects them. We follow the guest back down the hallway, closing and locking her bedroom door after we exit.

"It's present time!" Naomi yells in excitement as we reappear and make our way back to the party.

As she opens gifts, I notice my anxiety rising. I'm quickly

becoming overwhelmed by the crowd. It's time for me to go. I wait around long enough for Naomi to open the gift I brought before I announce I'll be retiring for the evening.

I slip out without further conversation and run for my car. Wasting no time, I throw the car into drive and before I know it, I'm on the highway headed back to the cabin. I haven't been home since I left. My parents alternate going by to check on things. All I do is pay the bills at this point. I'm not ready to go home just to be alone, to be without Noah.

The soft tunes of Luther Vandross distract me until I'm met with orange flashing lights up ahead. There's a detour sign ahead that wasn't there when I came through earlier. With no option but to take the detour, I follow a long line of vehicles down an alternate route. At first, I'm a bit lost as to where the detour is taking us but I see something familiar that serves as an indicator of my location. As I realize where I am, my anxiety rises. My headlights highlight what many may call a midnight ribbon, a marker placed on the side of the road to let others know that a loved one was lost due to a driving accident in that exact spot. I come to a complete stop as my heart feels as if it's about to burst through my chest. I'm immediately flooded with unpleasant memories of Noah once more.

March 2020

I pace the floor with excited, waiting for Noah to return home from a weekend trip. He promised me a date night. In anticipation of his arrival, I've decorated the house quite nicely, lighting tea candles, bringing out our favorite snacks and wine, and cooking his favorite dinner. I topped that off with freshly picked roses from the bush just outside the back patio. Since moving in together this has been one of the best ways to spend date night. And it feels so damn good to finally be Mrs. Noah Richardson.

To make the occasional even more special, I pulled out his favorite tablecloth. It was gifted to us by his mother for our wedding. She said she and my father-in-law used it during the first meal they had in their very first home. It was given to her by her mother, so a family heirloom that Noah and I vowed to take care of. This wouldn't be our first meal together, but one of our firsts in our new house that we purchased together just before the wedding. Considering the tablecloth is white trimmed in gold makes it perfect for the occasion, as our plates, glasses, and silverware have a similar resemblance.

Expecting Noah to arrive at any time, I pull dinner from the oven and prepare our plates, pouring up our favorite wine and lighting the last bit of candles. I dim the lights and check the time once more on my cell. With no calls or messages from him, I can only suspect his phone is either dead or he's trying to surprise me. Either way, I'm just excited to see my man.

Growing impatient, I attempt to call Noah. The phone line trills and goes to voicemail. I can twice more and send a text. Hopefully, he'll turn up soon. Not wanting the food to get cold, I move to place the food in the oven until he arrives when I notice one of the motion sensor lights around the front of the townhome kick on. Filled with excitement, I make haste to the front door. Passing the living room window, I see a silhouette I know all too well. I quicken my steps, bare feet clapping against the cool wood floors.

"Baby! You're home!" I fling the door open.

The sight before me is not what I expected upon greeting Noah.

His towering, muscular build now appears frail and battered as he collapses to the ground before me.

"Noah! Noah!" I let out a gut-wrenching scream. "No, no, no, no! Baby! What's wrong? What happened?"

My knees skid across the pavement as I stoop to his level, examining his body, urging him to respond. His words are few and incoherent, so getting him to explain what's happened doesn't seem likely. Unsure of what to do or how to stop the bleeding, the only thing I know to do is scoop him into my arms, like a baby. That's when I realized his condition was much worse than I could have imagined. His beautiful, expresso hued complexion is badly scarred and draping from his face. His skin is literally peeling from his body. As I examine him further, I realize his clothing is torn to hell and he's missing a shoe. I look out into the distance, at the driveway and the street, and I don't see his vehicle. My firs thought is that he'd gotten into an accident on his way home. That would explain the missed calls and messages.

"G-Grace...Ggg...Grace," my name comes out of his mouth along with gurgling blood.

"Baby, please don't leave me. Just hang on. I'm gonna call for help!" I cry out, attempting not to panic, attempting to be strong for him. "Baby, just stay with me. I'm gonna go in the house and get my phone so we can get you some—"

"Shh...just...just stay with me," he utters through ragged breaths.

"Please, let me go call for help,"' I try to release him from my embrace but he stops me.

"Stay with me," he groans, struggling to speak.

In a nervous panic, I let out a scream as one last plea for help and one of my neighbors across the street flick on their porch light.

"Grace? Everything ok? What's happening?"

49

"Noah's been hurt! Please call 911!"

My neighbor scrambles into the house and returns with a cordless phone, screaming to the 911 operator for help.

"I'm not gonna make it, I can feel it," he speaks.

"Don't say that. Stay with me! Please!"

His body proceeds to make sudden jerking movements and his breaths become shorter.

"I...love...you...Grace..."

"No, none of that! Help is on the way, you're gonna be fine. Just stay away and don't move. Help is coming." I work to reassure him but the stillness of his body and chilling look in his eyes tells me otherwise.

I hear the sirens in the distance.

"See, I told you help was on the way. You're gonna be alright."

As the sirens approach and the wailing takes over, I wave my arms in the air signaling for help. But when I look back down at Noah and his eyes are locked on me.

"You're forever my girl. My love. My life. My everything." He let it all out in one breath, his final breath. Right there in my arms, I watch him take his last breath.

When reality hits me, when I realize that he's gone, I completely lose my shit.

"You don't get to die on me, dammit! We were supposed to have more time!" I squeal and sob uncontrollably. As newlyweds of less than a year, this was a fear we once discussed and now that fear has become a reality. My best friend, my husband, the love of my life is gone. He's just...gone.

As the paramedics pry him from my arms, his last words echo throughout my body, haunting me.

It wasn't until a few days later I found out through investigation that Noah was hit by a drunk driver who veered into oncoming traf-

fic. He swerved to try and miss Noah, and he did, but Noah's car went off the road and into the ravine off a small two-lane road not too far from our neighborhood.

I snap back to reality only to be met by the sight of the midnight ribbon takes the cake and my eyes become flushed with tears. Unable to control my emotions or the thoughts surrounding the night of his accident, I follow the line of traffic until there's a clearing. I pull over and put the car in park. I rip the seatbelt away from my body in order to decrease the sensation of claustrophobia that's quickly paralyzing my body, making it hard to breathe.

And if tonight hasn't been triggering enough, our favorite song, *Angel of Mine* by Monica begins to play.

"Why are you teasing me? Why, God?" I roar to the heavens as tears flee my eyes, cascading down my face and onto my chest.

Using the breathing methods recommended by my therapist, I gradually calm myself. Merging back into traffic, I continue following the detour until I'm routed back to the main road. In no time, I arrive at the lake house. It's the only place I feel safe. It's become my emotional haven.

FIVE

*S*eeing the therapist on a regular schedule again has somewhat helped. I've been learning tactics to hold myself together when I'm about to fall into a crying tangent. I decided staying at my house for now was too much, so I've been holed up in the lake house and gave it a face lift. My parents bought this house in the late nineties, and a lot of the décor needed to be upgraded, like the wallpaper, the furniture, and, not to mention, the doors. I've given it a more modern look.

The flowers in the garden are in full bloom. The yard maintenance has been taking up most of my time, but it's giving me a sense of fulfillment. Along with gardening, I've taken up crafting. I've gotten pretty good at scrapbooking and crocheting if I may say so myself.

For some reason, today just seems like the perfect day for fishing. I'll admit, I haven't fished in years and my Dad was normally the one to bait and unhook my fish from the line, but something about fishing today just seemed pleasant. While a don't have fishing supplies on hand, I remember there's a bait and tackle shop not too far from the lake house.

"Hey Marve!" I speak, waving at the store owner. Marve has owned this store since I was a little girl. His father owned it before him, and his father's father before that. I love shopping with small family businesses.

"Hey, Grace. Good to see ya. Anything I can help you find today?"

I'm thankful I have a hat on my head today. There are a lot more people than usual in the store, and I'm a bit uncomfortable.

"Marve, don't worry about me. I just need a few things to go fishing. I can find it."

"I don't mind helping. You're one of my favorites," Marve says over his shoulder. He's facing the two-way mirror. I look into it, to see what has his attention, and there's a woman on the first aisle who looks completely lost.

"I'm sure. I got it, Marve, thanks."

He nods and makes his way to the woman. I find myself on the third aisle, known for different types of bait, depending on what you're hunting. I had no idea the many different variations of all the fish inside the lake, so I went with the most common one—dried flies and a few algae poppers. I've been using the same pole my entire life. It was my father's and his father's, another reason why I'm a fan of family items and stores.

By the time I get what I need, Marve is back up at the store counter, ready to check me out. As always, Marve gives me a smile as he checks me out, and I'm on my way almost as quickly as I arrived.

Arriving back at the lake house, I'm met by a parked car in the exact spot that I've been parking in for weeks now. But it's not just any car, it's my parent's car. I park parallel to them, taking a deep breath stepping out of the car. I've been doing ok lately but I also realize I need to prepare myself to possibly hear more of my mother's forced ideas about how I should grieve and what I should be doing with my life instead. Let us pray she's in a good mood today.

My feet drag as I make my way to the door, but when I step inside, both of my parents had kind smiles on their faces. It isn't that my mother is some evil bitch, I know that she loves me, but she has a side to her that comes across as heartless and inconsiderate.

"Hi, sweetheart. We decided to stop by for a chat," my mother speaks first, her hands reaching out for mine. I place my bag from the bait and tackle shop on the floor by the front door and reach out to her.

"It's nice to see you, and you too, Daddy, but it would've been nice if you would've called first." I smile back politely, but I mean what I'm saying.

"Well, I didn't think you'd let us come if we called first. Here, sit. I want to talk to you really quick."

I follow her lead and settle on the couch beside her.

"I need to apologize, Grace, for my behavior a few months ago."

Though my mother's words sound sincere, I'm not ready to accept them. A moment of silence passes between us. I'm not ready to accept what she has to say right now.

"Daddy, since you're here, would you like to fish a little? I planned to hit the lake." I completely avoid my mother's conversation, redirecting the conversation to something lighter. I know that I can easily get Dad's attention by mentioning fishing.

"Of course, sweetheart. I'd love to." My father nods. I let go of my mother's hands, grab the bag, and head toward the back door where the dock quietly awaits us.

"I'll set the grill up and get it going for when you two get back," my mother calls to our backs. I don't say a word, I just keep moving with my father.

Stepping out onto the deck, the pressure and tension I felt from my mother's presence fades almost instantly.

We load Dad's trusted johnboat with the necessary gear for fishing and we climb into the boat. Just as I did as a small girl, I start the motor.

"To the middle?" I ask, looking up at my father.

"Absolutely. Just like I taught you, pumpkin."

I nod, and wen begin to glide across the lake, heading toward the middle.

Forty minutes of small chitchat go by, and we've caught more than enough for dinner, but I'm hesitant to return. My father can sense it, I can tell.

"Are you really that mad at your mother? Don't you think you've been holding the attitude a bit too long, baby?"

I look up from my pole hesitantly, glancing up at my father. He's a good man; he always has been. I know as much as he loves me, he loves my mom, and he always tries to have her back when he can.

"Daddy, I'm not mad at her. I'm just disappointed. I hoped she would've been more considerate of my feelings. Even you were upset with her, remember?" I ask, shrugging my shoulders.

"I was upset. I felt much like you, that she should have more compassion, but I know your mother, and I understand where she's coming from. If you'd given her a moment, she could've explained this to you herself. But you always let your emotions dictate everything about you."

I'm shocked to hear my father say this.

"Can you blame me? My husband—"

"I know. I was fond of Noah, and I know how much he meant to you. I think her delivery was poor, but what she was saying has a lot of merit. I think you should give your mother another chance. Now let's get back before it starts to get dark. Your mother has been waiting long enough."

Maybe Dad is right. Maybe I did overreact a bit but at the same time my feelings are my own and everyone processes things differently. I just expected her to understand more. I just wanted her to understand my situation as if it were hers, as if it was her husband. One thing I've learned over time, people don't see the relevance nor understand a situation until it hits home for them. Either way, I think I can take the first step toward clearing the air with my mother.

"So, are you going to give her a chance to explain?" my father asks as we both stand to get out of the boat. I grab onto his hand and step up onto the dock first. He follows behind me.

"I'll hear what she has to say. I didn't like what you had to say at first, but I'll listen."

My father throws his arm around my shoulders and leans down to kiss me on the forehead.

"Don't apologize to me. Apologize to mom. I'm gonna clean the fish and cook while you and Mom have a talk."

As we return, Mom is standing, waiting for our return.

"Look what we got, baby! I caught three, but Grace caught two. Her contribution is noted."

Dad smiles, and Mom brings her hands up to her lips. "Of course, she did. Good job, Grace. I've got everything set up in the kitchen for you, baby. You mind leaving me and Grace out here for a second?"

Before I let my father speak up, I say, "I actually wanted to talk to you anyway. Me and Mom will get the sides together Dad. You take care of the rest?" I suggest as I take a seat at the patio table.

"Of course. You two go ahead." Dad kisses Mom on the cheek and goes into the house, no doubt getting ready to do his thing with the fish.

The moment we're left alone and I turn my attention to Mom, I can feel the nervousness and tension between us. She takes a seat across from me, letting out a sigh. She's quiet, and I'm unsure of what to say, but somehow, we both end up speaking at the same time.

"Mom—"

"Grace, I—"

We both smile, and I sit back. "You go ahead and go, Mom."

The sun is going down, the sky is just turning pink. It feels serene and the perfect setting to have this conversation.

"I'm gonna be honest. I was raised during a time where expressing yourself and your emotions made you vulnerable. It made you someone who was a target. I know times have changed, and I know things are different. It was odd to fall apart during my time, and it made me stronger to keep pushing. I assumed it would give you purpose if you kept going. I don't want you to lose all you've worked for, which is why I encouraged you to return to work. I didn't mean to be insensitive. I'm sorry, sweetheart."

I understand where my mother is coming from and I have the utmost respect for her. I guess it's just a matter of me realizing that there are generational differences at play. She didn't raise me to be hard, to be insensitive thought and I've always been able to express myself, so it felt odd to me that my mother she silenced me before. This reminds me of a message I listened to last year, mentioning how though we've grown up and moved on that doesn't necessarily mean we've healed from it. When these things go unattended, unhealed, they tend to become triggered unexpectedly. I wonder if my situation triggered some unresolved feelings around the death of my grandparents. My mother never had the time to heal. She went from being a kid to being a parent overnight.

Not wanting to stir any feelings, I choose a simpler reply.

"I'm sorry, too. I wasn't expecting you to respond to me the way you did regarding his death but now I understand why you reacted the way you did."

Mom's face lights up, and tears fill the rims of her eyes. I can tell our rift has been hard on her. I've been ignoring her phone calls and only responding to text messages. Forgiving her was easier once we had a conversation.

Through the window, I see Dad's face. He can't hear what we're saying, but he can see the sentiment in the air. The tension has clearly been cut.

"Now, since we're being open with one another, I need to

have another conversation with you, honey. Why don't you follow me into the house and meet me in the master bathroom, ok?"

I have a confused look on my face, but I nod my head anyway, wondering what my mother wants with me in the bathroom. I let her go ahead of me, and I follow closely behind.

Mom places her large black Gucci purse onto the bathroom counter and she pulls the chair from the vanity over closer to me.

"Have a seat sweetheart." Mom pats the back of cushion of the chair, wanting me to sit down. I don't question it; I just take a seat. But when she starts reaching for my cap, my heart starts pounding.

"Mama, don't—"

"Shh…it's ok. I'm Mama, I'll make sure you're ok."

She kisses the side of my cheek as she removes the cap from my head. I've maintained the length of my hair, but the thickness is a thing of the past. I have several bald spots and patches where my hair doesn't grow quite right anymore. Shame fills me. It seems like I'm under a microscope.

"So, I brought along some of my hair products. I'm sixty years old and have hair like a nineteen-year-old because of this stuff right here."

My mother reaches down into her purse and pulls out a jar of Castor oil and coconut oil. She has a silk bonnet, large enough to be a chef's hat.

"I'm gonna grease your scalp, and then put this bonnet on, baby. You've got to start taking care of your hair if you want to keep it, ok?" Mom's voice is gentle. She isn't overstepping. Her concern is genuine.

"Ok," I say, as my voice whimpers.

Mom pulls out her comb and begins sectioning my hair off into four parts. She hums as she does it and my heart melts. I can literally feel some of the sadness I've been carrying being replaced with love, with warmth, with sincerity. I feel as if the shame I've held of the condition of my hair is gone. I hate that my mother worries so much, and I've made her worry. I have to be honest with myself and say that the stress has me losing weight and not taking care of myself as I should. I'm thinner than usual, but I'm making progress. My therapist made it clear that I need to take in the progression, even if it seems small to me. A small victory for me right now has not been wishing to be dead. The hole in my chest doesn't feel as large as it did a month ago.

"Now, go ahead and shower and get the lake off of you and join us for dinner."

Before I can stand up from my seat, my father appears in the doorway. "Dinner is ready whenever you ladies are ready to eat, and tonight, you're going to eat, ok?" Dad suggested, but I know what he's hinting to. I'm not the only person who's noticed my weight loss.

"I will, just let me shower and I'll meet you both downstairs."

"Alright, just remember, taking care of yourself, whether it's a shower, a bath, or even just getting a pedicure, that has to be your priority, ok sweetheart?" Dad asks and leaves me with a kiss on the cheek.

Today has been a good day, and I'm looking forward to eating dinner with my parents now that we've cleared the air. My scalp feels amazing, and it smells good too. I'm going to have to look into getting some of those products my mom used on me today. My shower is quick, because the finished dinner has the entire house smelling like it should be eaten, and I have a bit of an appetite tonight. I look over at my phone that's lounging on the nightstand, and I've been in the shower a little over an hour. Rushing now, now that it mattered, I quickly dry off and throw on something presentable. I pull my hair back into a simple bun and don't waste a minute more.

My feet hit the hallway, running to meet my parents at the table, but there's a note on it that reads,

We waited for you for as long as we could, but we had to get back to the city. Your father has a big meeting in the morning, and I have a hair appointment that's non-refundable. We love you. Call us soon.

A smile appears on my face as I stroke my fingertips across the index card the note was left on. It was nice seeing them, but it was also nice to have the house back. Suddenly, I find myself thirsty, so I make myself a large glass of cranberry juice from the fridge. Next to the bottle of cranberry juice, I notice Dad's left me a plate covered with saran wrap. I take the plate as well, putting it in the microwave to bring some warmth to the food.

I reopen the fridge to place the juice inside, and as I close the refrigerator door, something silver catches my attention. I've been here several weeks now and I've never noticed this until today. Tucked tightly between the cabinet and the refrigerator is a two-sided silver piece of cardstock. It's a Save the Date announcement for me and Noah's wedding. Mom and Dad were visiting the lake house when these were sent out.

I lean down to pick it up, and the memory of our wedding day floods my memory as I lose my balance. I grip onto the sink's edge, and let the moment take me.

September 2018

"Grace Marie Middleton, I will love you until the day I die. I'll love you when I'm in Heaven, and I'll save you a seat right next to me. I'll love you when your hair is gray and when your teeth fall out. You're my forever, love eternal. We've spent enough time apart, and here today, in front of our family, God, and all of our friends, I proclaim that I'll never leave you, I'll never forsake you, and I promise to be yours, until the end of time."

The entire audience is in shock hearing Noah's vows to me, as am I. I know he loves me but hearing him say it like this in front of everyone gives me vibes I've never felt before. I hold onto my stomach, hoping my emotions don't break free. We spent so much on pictures; I'd hate for them to get ruined with my tears.

"I now pronounce you husband and wife. You may now, kiss your bride," the wedding officiant announces. One minute, I'm standing on my feet, and the next minute, Noah has me snatched up in his arms, my feet dangling over his arms as he kisses me passionately, letting the entire world know that I'm his.

My hand is on my heaving chest. Tears are falling from my eyes, and a scream is on the verge from escaping me. As I hold myself over the sink, my heart singing me the blues, I hear something, a thump. I figure my mom and dad have decided not to leave after all, or maybe they left something.

"Mom, Dad?" I call out, waiting for someone to respond to

me. I stand still for a moment as I look over my shoulder, but I don't hear anything, and I don't see anyone. I decide to grab the plate of fish and just take it to my room. I would rather eat in there anyway. I'm walking down the hallway that leads to my bedroom, and I hear something again, another noise. My heart starts to pound as paranoia sets in. I've been staying here for quite some time and not once have I had issues with people or animals. Now, out of the blue, I'm hearing noises.

As quickly as possible, without running, I head in the direction of my bedroom, almost sliding into it, and the noise persists. I throw the fish plate onto the dresser and reach for my handgun. My father, thank goodness, kept the house protected, and he taught me how to protect myself.

From my room, I can see the living room, and the shadows within it. By the window that overlooks the lake, I see a figure...a person. I raise my gun and walk along the wall, stretching my arms outward in the event I need to let off a shot.

"I'm armed, and I'm not afraid to shoot. If you want to live, you should leave and never bother me again!" I warn. I want to make sure before I blow whoever this is to pieces, they know what's coming for them so they can make the right decision and just leave.

The closer I get to the living room; I see the shadowy figure getting closer. I would be an idiot to think I would get a shot off toward this person unless they came out of the dark. But the closer I get, and the closer they get, their body is outlined under the light of the moon. Denim jeans come into view, with a t-shirt with a picture of Jimi Hendrix on the front, and a pair of Steve Madden Kramerr tan leather boots. I know that outfit; I'm the one who purchased it last year.

"Is this a joke?" my voice is more elevated than I'm used to, but this must be some twisted and sick prank. The man moves toward me, his hands up as a sign of surrender. Now that he's in the light, I can see him clear as day. My mouth falls open as the gun falls from my hands and hits the ground with a loud thump.

"Grace, if you'll let me explain, I promise, it's me. It's Noah."

My feet feel stuck in place. I can't scream, I can't move. I've lost all motor capability. The man who looks like Noah comes closer to me, backing me into the wall. Our faces are just inches away from one another. The Noah doppelganger reaches up, extending his hand toward my face. I back further into the wall, trying to bring more distance between us, but his hand graces my fact anyway.

It's a touch I never thought I'd feel again, as goosebumps riddle my body. I cradle my face in his hand, taking in the full-ness of the moment. When I'm sure this isn't a dream, I place my hand over his heart, just to see if it's really beating, if he really lives. His heartbeat is as strong as it was the last time I laid my head on his chest. It was always the perfect rhythm to fall asleep to.

"I-it's really you?" My hand flies to my mouth. The shock is almost enough to make me faint.

He nods, and I oddly enough I feel complete. Nothing else in the world matters, except I have him back in my life. I leap into his arms, afraid he won't catch me, but I don't care. I miss him so much that his presence alone is enough.

"I told you, I'd never let you fall," his deep, sensuous voice graces my ears. That only causes me to cry incessantly.

65

SIX

*W*ith no words to exchange, Noah picks me up and carries me back to the bedroom. We kiss one another like it's the last time we'll ever kiss again. We haven't touched one another in so long, but our bodies remember one another as though no time has passed. Tenderly, Noah tosses me on the bed, leaving a trail of kisses from my neck to my chest. Unable to contain himself, he begins to rip my clothes from my body.

"Noah, I love you…" comes out as a whisper, though in my head I'm shouting.

"I love you too, Grace."

Noah's hands inch up and down my body, creating tiny bits of explosions inside and out. At the sight of Noah, I'm ready to give myself to him as I did when we first made love. I open my thighs, inviting Noah to nestle himself between them. Before he approaches me, he works to quickly unbutton his jeans. And when he does, his manhood hangs there at the opening, just as I remember. Wanting him now more than ever, I tug at his forearm, begging him to come closer. Tears are still falling, I'm ready to be loved. Without hesitation, Noah plunges inside me.

"NOAH!" I bellow. He completely caught me off guard.

While the entry is a bit painful, the pain quickly subsides and the pleasure kicks in. Captivated by the feel of him, his presence, I take a backseat and my body takes control. I engulf him in my embrace, extending my arms around his back, my nails raking down the center of his spine.

Noah crashes into my center, time and time again, causing my breasts bounce freely with delight as our bodies collide. The deeper he penetrates me, the tighter I wrap my legs around his waist, squeezing him into me. We make love like we never have before, taking me into a full state of euphoria as our bodies meld together fluently. I try several times but he doesn't allow me to take control. Instead, he leaves me in the missionary position, pleasuring me in any way possible until I climax. My climax is followed by his, as he leaves his essence inside me. With no communication for what's just occurred, we curl up to one another and fall asleep in one another's embrace for the first time in months.

The next morning, I wake to a cold chill on my right arm. Clearing my vision, I realize the blanket is on the floor. I look to my left, and I find an empty space. Immediate disappoint takes over me as I realize everything about Noah from last night was nothing more than a dream. What even more disappointing is the fact that I'd never dreamt of him so realistically before. I set into instant panic, disappointed in the fact that I've allowed myself to get to this point. Just when I thought I was handling his death better, now comes this. My head drops between my shoulders and I release a deep sigh.

"Good morning baby," a voice speaks.

My eyes spring upward and I find Noah standing in the doorway of the bedroom.

"You're still here…" my breathing begins to slow.

"Of course. Where else would I be? Grace, baby, are you ok?"

"Yeah, no, I don't know. I'm so confused."

"Confused? Confused about what?" He moves from the doorway, creeping toward me. Eventually, he rests at the foot of the bed.

I hate to ruin the mood, but I have questions that need answers.

"Noah, I need to know some things. Like, how and why are you here?" I inquire. Hopefully, he'll be straightforward with me.

When he speaks, his voice is deeper and smoother than I remember. His eyes are inviting, and his smile is warm.

"I'm here for you…."

His words lock me in a trance, and I'm drawn back to his body. I scoot down the bed, closer to him. He places his hands around my head and gently squeezes. Everything I want to know can wait. What can't wait is the fire between us that can only be extinguished when we make love. His lips pursue mine heavily, as he leans me back against the bed. I'm back in the center, where I started the morning, and where I would be put to bed, once again.

When I wake up from my sex induced coma, and the clock on the nightstand is set. I never set the clock before because the time hasn't been important to me. Every second seemed to linger too long. The only time I look at the time on my phone is when necessary, but now that Noah is back, he's already settling back into his old routine. He doesn't believe in relying on the time on your phone. He instead always sets the clocks around the house. The microwave, the wall clock, and the clock on the nightstand as well.

I swing my legs over the bed, eager to use the restroom and then get downstairs to whatever smells delicious. This afternoon is different than the others I've had. This afternoon, I can go into the kitchen, and Noah will be there. Every ounce of sadness has melted away with his arrival, but my unanswered still linger.

After a quick shower, I grab my robe hanging on the back of the bathroom door and walk barefoot to my destination. On my way down the hall, the aroma of the food permeates my nose. I take a deep breath, ready to embrace the fact that my husband is somehow back from the dead.

"Good afternoon." His voice awakens me and covers me like a blanket.

"Good afternoon," I reply, tilting onto my tippy toes, leaving Noah with a kiss on the cheek. "You're cooking already?" I ask as I examine the beautiful spread he's made. He's prepared us turkey avocado sandwiches with fried egg and bacon on rye bread. It looks delicious.

"Of course, after last night and this morning, I figured you could use it." He shrugs his shoulders as he pulls my chair out for me at the table. Sitting down, I waste no time taking a bite of the meal he's prepared.

"You are right about that. I'm worn out. I haven't had that much physical exertion in months."

Though I'm trying hard not to ruin the mood, I keep getting the nudge to speak up.

"So, I know you didn't say much before, and I didn't press, but now I need to know. Why are you really here? How long will you be here? I know you're dead, and I know I'm not crazy, so how can I touch you? Did God finally feel sorry for me and decide to give you back? Is this somehow a second chance? Am I—"

Noah's hand slides over mine, and I'm quieted for a moment. He adjusts himself in his seat. He's wearing his jeans, with no t-shirt.

"I'm here...for you, my love." He squeezes my hand gently. His embrace is so wanted, I accept another depthless answer. With that, I decide to finish my lunch. The only thing I want to do is spend time with my husband, to be in his loving arms, to be near him. Nothing else matters.

"Your garden is beautiful. It's nice that you've kept it up."

Noah and I are outside, taking a break from all the love making we've been doing. Since he's come back, it's almost the only thing we do. I can't get enough of him. We cuddle all day and reminisce about old times, reminding one another of how deeply we love and have missed one another.

"Thank you, the garden is the only thing that keeps me up."

Noah's hand touches my cheek and I lean into it. My heart is full.

"I'm sure you're proud of it. It's really blooming," Noah acknowledges, catching my attention.

"You're so loving and considerate," I gush. I'm so happy that he's pleased with what I've done in his absence. I always loved to garden, but I guess I loved it more once he was gone. It's kept me together and given me a routine since I stopped going to work. It's been a week, and I haven't spoken to my therapist. I don't feel like I need to tell anyone about what's going on right now. At least not my therapist. She, at times, seems a bit judgmental, and I want to enjoy spending time with him before I have to give him back to the world.

Noah's hand now in mine, he turns us back around to face the house. We go back inside, and he looks at the couch that faces the fireplace.

"Let's make some s'mores, like old times!" Noah suggests with excitement.

"Let's go for it. I think I have enough chocolate for us to make quite a few. C'mon," I take his hand, leading him to the kitchen.

As I begin, Noah suggests hot chocolate. He loves hot chocolate, and despite the nearly 80-degree weather, he'll still drink it.

In not time, the s'mores and hot chocolate are done and ready to be consumed. The pure joy on his face while eating and drinking is priceless.

The next day was much of the same. Noah and I were in the middle of kissing, headed into another sex trance, when my stomach starts to turn again. I know I'm going to vomit. I haven't had an episode in two weeks, but now, I feel nauseous again. I grab the sheet, since I'm naked, and rush to the bathroom. I hear footsteps moving around as I'm throwing my guts up.

"Grace, Grace! Are you ok?" I look over my shoulder to find Naomi standing in my bedroom.

"Wh-what are you doing here?" I ask as I wipe off my mouth and flush the toilet.

"I came to check on you. Grace, your vomit is green. Are you ok?"

"I've honestly never been better. Give me a second." I put my finger up and pull the door closed a bit so I can wash my hands and swish my mouth out with water. When I'm finished, I open the bathroom door, and Naomi has a worried look on her face.

"I'm fine, really. Just not feeling well, but I'm ok."

"Ok, well at least let me help you get dressed. You don't look well. I really want you to see a doctor."

"I really am fine, but you can help me get dressed," I say, realizing I do feel a little weak.

Naomi places the sacks she's carrying down and walks me over to my closet. I'm anxious for her to leave so that I can get back to Noah, wherever he disappeared to. In the closet, I sit down on the foot stool and wait for her to pick out an outfit for me.

Waiting for her to decide, I sit nauseated. Naomi extends my legs to help me put on a pair of peach leggings, that I have a matching shirt to. Naomi and I have been friends for so long,

I'm not uncomfortable being naked in front of her. She reaches for my arms and raise them for me.

"Keep your arms up so we can slide your shirt on. I'm gonna stay the night, and tomorrow, I'm taking you to the doctor. You haven't been feeling well for weeks, and I'm really starting to worry."

I shrug my shoulders, knowing that she doesn't understand how I'm feeling. I really do feel fine. A little throw up is normal.

Once I'm dressed, I climb back into bed. My stomach is still turning, but I don't want to give Naomi any extra reason to worry, so I comply to her request. My covers are on the floor, filled with love from Noah and I, but they're the only thing I want to lay in. Naomi pulls the blanket over me and tells me to rest.

The moment Naomi leaves my room, I feel sleep coming over me. I'm tired, and my eyes start to flutter shut. It's best not to fight the sleep, so I just let it take me.

Several hours later, I wake up to find Noah's arm around me. I'm feeling better already. I look up into his face, and he's got a glow about him. It makes my stomach pain flee.

"I slept so well. Come on, let's go into the living room and go see Naomi. She'll be thrilled to see you."

Noah's face seems troubled, but I'm sure he's just worried about all the questions.

"Don't worry. You don't have to tell her anything." I smile and reach for his hand. He takes mine and we go out into the hallway, where we see Naomi bending over one of my potted plants that needs to be clipped.

"Hey, Naomi!" I say, a little more excited than I normally would.

"Hey, it's good to see you on your feet. How was your nap?"

My arm is swinging with Noah's hand in mine, waiting for Naomi to acknowledge Noah.

"It was great, thanks to you, and to Noah." I tilt my head in his direction, waiting for her to say something about the fact that Noah is right beside me.

"Noah? How did Noah help?" Naomi asks, now facing me completely. Her body is turned upright.

"He always makes everything better. He cuddled me while I was asleep. His warmth just soothed me, I guess you could say."

Naomi's eyebrows furrow. She looks like she's about to pass out.

"Naomi, what's wrong?"

Moving closer to me, she covers her mouth and looks at me intensely. Something is obviously bothering her. She hasn't even said anything about Noah yet.

"Well, for starters, the fact that you think your husband was cuddling you. Maybe you mean with his shirt. Were you cuddling with his shirt? Something of his?"

My neck is craned looking at Naomi. She has to be kidding.

"Are you serious right now? No, not his clothes. It's Noah. He's here." Our hands are still locked.

"Fine, if he's here, tell him to come out here, to come and see me. He knows me…"

"He's right here! That's what I'm saying. See?" I step to the side and move my arms up and down, presenting him to

Naomi. Naomi's shaking her head, and I know she doesn't believe me.

"Alright, since you don't believe me, look at these. I've got love marks all over my body. We've been having sex like mad teenagers!" I'm shouting with frustration. I can't believe she's acting like she doesn't see what's happening here.

"Those are bruises, and even more reason for you to go to the doctor! I'm taking you tomorrow whether you want to go or not!"

Tears form in my eyes. Noah's hand is now on my shoulder, comforting me. His warmth is all I need to get through. For some reason, Naomi doesn't understand. She's not being supportive. I shake my head and turn around.

"I'll see you in the morning when it's time to go to the doctor's office, Naomi."

"Well, wait, don't you want to eat? I'm sorry, I didn't mean to upset you."

I stop for a moment to think about what I want to say. "I'm not upset. I'll be fine. I'm not hungry. I'm gonna just go to my room and relax with Noah."

She doesn't say anything as I make my way back to my room with Noah beside me. I'm not even in the mood to argue or keep exhausting myself. Instead, I crawl into bed, and Noah gets in beside me, comforting me once again.

Like the blink of an eye, one day rolls into another. I wake to hearing Naomi downstairs moving around. Noah is still asleep, so I don't want to wake him. Besides, I'll just tell him about the appointment when I get back. I go ahead and get ready, opting to put on a pair of jeans and white tee.

"So glad you're awake. I was gonna come check on you in a minute. We can leave in like twenty minutes. I need to finish my coffee and grab my bag and put on my shoes."

I just nod. I'm not mad at Naomi but having to have the "Noah conversation" with her again would be draining, and I'd like to refrain from having it. Naomi disappears into the guestroom and I take a seat on the couch, just waiting for her to come back. I'm not going to lie, I'm a bit anxious about going to the doctor. I just pray that whatever it is can be fixed quickly. I've been feeling sick for too long.

"Ready?" Naomi reappears. I don't say anything, I just stand and follow her out of the house to the vehicle.

Slipping into the car, I'm glad that Naomi hasn't said a word to me. She cut the music on the second we clicked on our seat-belts. Things between Naomi and I have never been so strained. We normally can talk about everything, but right now, that's the last thing I want to do.

***

"Hello, I'd like to check in as a walk-in. I need to see Dr. Cohen if possible." The receptionist doesn't look up. She just sticks a clipboard out of the window and instructs me to fill it out.

I take a seat and Naomi positions herself across from me. She thinks I can't see her peeping over the paperwork. She's double checking my answers, shifting uncomfortably in her chair. I quickly fill out the papers, answering as many questions as I can remember the answers to, and then return the clip-board to the receptionist.

As I wait to be called to the back, I get the strong sense that Naomi wants to say something to me. Normally I would encourage her to do so, but I'm not in the mood for confrontation right now. My anxiety is through the roof thinking of the possibilities of what the doctor will say when I see him. I've been seeing Dr. Cohen for years. He's very familiar with my body and my medical history, which makes me feel comfortable enough to come in for a visit despite not wanting to come at all.

Thirty minutes pass, and I find myself on my way up to the desk to ask how much longer the wait might be, until the door opens and a nurse calls my name.

"Finally," I say aloud. Naomi jumps to her feet, almost as quickly as I do, and we head to the back to be seen. The nurse starts out by getting my weight and taking my blood pressure.

"It's a little low. Have you eaten today?" the nurse asks as she directs us to a room.

"I haven't. I don't have much of an appetite honestly."

Naomi gives me the side eye and the nurse lets out a cute "mmm" before leaving us alone in the patient room.

The silence between Naomi and I is stale. We have yet to exchange words. The silence is becoming too much, but I don't want to be the person to break the ice first, especially when I'm not sure where to start or what I really want to say.

Fortunately, the doctor arrives before either of us is forced to speak.

"Hey, Doctor Cohen, how are you?"

"I'm alright. How you doin' today, Grace? Who do you have with you today?" he asks, looking toward Naomi.

78

"This is Naomi, my best friend."

"I am, and I wanted her to come to the doctor today. I've got some concerns."

Looking over at Naomi, I roll my eyes. She has concerns, and so do I, but about two totally different things.

"Alright, well I looked over your chart, and before we run any tests, I want to just verify a few things. You've been experiencing hair loss, frequent vomiting, loss of appetite?"

I nod, confirming the details.

"Ok, I'd like to get urine and blood samples, and I'd also like to schedule a couple other scans so that we can get a look inside your stomach.

"Sure, how long do you think that will take? I'm kind of eager to get back home."

Naomi gives my statement a slight "tuh" and she crosses her legs in her seat.

"I'm sure you are. It shouldn't take more than about an hour. Don't worry. We'll do our best to get you in and out. I'll have the nurse in shortly and we'll get things started."

The doctor let's himself out and I realize I have to go ahead and say something to Naomi at this point.

"You know, Naomi, you might have your own opinion, and you're allowed to have it, but it's not cool that you keep trying to put me down. Noah is as real as you and I are. You'll see."

"Grace, you can't be—"

Naomi didn't get to finish her statement. The nurse unknowingly interrupts, giving me a small cup to provide a urine sample. Providing instructions, she leads me down the hallway to a private bathroom.

After leaving a urine sample and a blood test, it's time for me to undergo an ultrasound to make sure my digestive track is ok. I get onto the table, and the lights are low. For a moment, I feel soothed and the stress starts to fade away.

"Ok, this is going to be just a little cold," the technician says as she holds up the wand to the ultrasound machine.

I nod and raise my shirt so that she may apply gel to my belly. It is cool, but it's nice. I don't feel nauseous right now, so her pressing on my stomach doesn't feel bad.

"Alright," she says as she moves the wand around, looking for what, I'm not sure. After a few minutes of looking, a picture appears on the screen.

"This is your baby's head here. It's nice and round." The technician smiles at me, and my eyes widen.

"Baby's head?" I spring forward. I'm shocked. "I'm...I'm pregnant? How?"

"Yes ma'am. See, these are the baby's feet, and the baby's other arm is resting on the baby's stomach."

"H-how far along am I?" I quiz her, filled with nervousness and excitement. I can't keep my eyes off the baby. It makes so much sense now why I haven't neem feeling well.

"From the ultrasound and your paperwork, it seems like four months, just a little over sixteen weeks is right."

I think back to four months ago, before Noah passed away. I was ovulating right before his trip, and even though he was going to be gone just a weekend, I couldn't let him leave without reminding him of what he'd be leaving behind. I gave him the best I had that entire week. The possibility of becoming pregnant hadn't been a consideration of mine throughout all this.

"So, we're going to get you a prescription for prenatal vitamins, and I know the doctor wanted to talk to you about a few other concerns."

"Concerns?" I question, listening for any indication that something might be terribly wrong.

"Yes ma'am, but I'll let the doctor talk to you about that. Congratulations on your baby."

I smile, but on the inside, I feel overwhelmed and afraid. Afraid of something else being wrong. The technician helps me clean off and I head back to the room I was originally in with Naomi. Her eyes have worry in them, and I know I should take her fear away by telling her what's going on.

"Well, I'm pregnant."

I come in and flop back down on the table. I'm excited but don't feel too excited to tell her about it.

"Pregnant? Oh my God, Grace! That's wonderful news! What else did they say?"

"I'm waiting for the doctor to come in now and tell me about the rest of his concerns or if something else is going on."

"Ok, well no matter what, at least we got some great news today!"

Naomi's excitement is hard to ignore, and my attitude won't hold up with such great news surrounding us. For a moment, things feel normal. We talk about how I'm four months along. I tell her about the baby sucking its thumb, and most of all, how I want it to be a boy. In the middle of us talking, the doctor comes back in with a dull look on his face.

"Alright, well first, I want to congratulate you on your pregnancy, Grace. This is your first baby?" Doctor Cohen asks, though he knows the answer. I nod.

"Thank you. It definitely explains why I've been throwing

up so much," I proclaim, rubbing my belly, thinking of the life growing inside me.

"True, but it doesn't explain the weight loss, the hair loss, and it shouldn't have made her that sick, right?" Naomi interjects, looking up at Doctor Cohen, waiting for a response.

"Exactly, which brings me to my next point. Grace, I'll be blunt with this. There's a growth on your pancreas, and it could be the primary cause of your late symptoms. I'd like to get you admitted so we can run a few more tests."

Every happy feeling evades me. To say I'm shocked is an understatement. Finding out I have a tumor growing inside completely takes away from the fact that I just learned I'm carrying Noah's seed.

"So, what's next?" I ask, and I extend my hand to Naomi, who without hesitation takes it, ready to be there to comfort me.

SEVEN

*I*t takes me a minute to wrap my mind around what needs to happen. It sounds like the doctor is speaking in Spanish with all the medical terms he's spewing. The one thing that stands out the most to me is the immediate laparoscopy I'll need to undergo. The doctor wraps up his explanations and asks if I need him to clarify anything. I say I understand but, truthfully, I don't. Naomi is by my side, but I feel lonely. I want…no…need Noah by my side. This is entirely too much for me to carry on my own. I want nothing more than to go home right now and allow him to hold me until this nightmare subsides.

"We're going to put you to sleep, so you won't feel a thing." Dr. Cohen explains. Despite his explanations, I'm scared shitless. Everything's happening so fast. "We'll insert a fiber-optic instrument through the abdominal wall so we can better look at what's happening, the best course of treatment, and so on. It won't take long, so just hang tight, and we'll get you into the OR."

Doctor Cohen's explanation makes me feel worse. I've never been put under, not even for a dental procedure. Doctor Cohen leaves me and Naomi in the room. I can tell she wants to say something, but like me, she isn't sure of what to say.

I'm sitting on the exam table, patting my foot impatiently, when Naomi takes a stance right before me. She wraps her arms around me, and I feel safe enough to release the fear, the tear that I've been harboring. What about my baby? What am I supposed to do about this now? Am I going to have to have extensive surgery? Just thinking about it all is making me weak.

A scream rips through my body. I'm so fed up with everything. This has truly been the worst year of my life, and I feel like no one on this planet can understand what I'm feeling. I calm down a bit once the nurse knocks on the door. She returns with a gown and sheer blue bonnet for my hair. I'm practically ready for surgery. Per the nurses' instructions, I remove my clothing, place it into a bag, and give it to Naomi for safekeeping.

"Listen, everything is going to be ok. I'm going to be here when you get out. I'm going to call your parents and have them come down here."

"No, you can't tell them. They'll just flip out and make things worse. I can't stand to see them hurt."

Naomi places my clothes down in the chair and takes my hands in hers.

"I know you're scared, but the worst thing you can do is keep this secret to yourself. If you do, it will only make matters worse. You're not the only person who needs to be informed, nor am I. Your parents will want to be here for you, so please let them."

I'm not as strong as I want to believe I am. I always crack under extreme pressure, and right now, I feel weak and helpless. My parents coming might only make things worse, but after them visiting, I don't want to leave them out. Mom made it clear that she's dedicated to being here for me. Naomi is right, she does need to get in contact with them. Anything could happen to me while I'm under heavy anesthesia.

"You're right. Get in contact with them and see if they're available to come."

With me securely laid out on an operating table, Naomi leans into me, leaving a kiss on my cheek. Though she's my best friend, at times, she's like a sister. She's always had my back, and even though we aren't seeing eye to eye right now, I appreciate her willingness to make and keep my comfortable during this process. She's seen me through so many things, and right now, she's going to see me through this procedure.

Hours have passed by, and I'm out of the procedure. I have no updates and don't know what's going on. My mother and father have been pacing the room, anxiously awaiting news, some news, any news, just as I have. The longer it takes, the more worried I become. I'm scared the news is going to be worse than I could have imagined, and this might not be a simple fix.

In a recovery room, I silently pray as I slip in and out of consciousness, begging God to give me another chance. I just want my baby to have a chance at a healthy life.

Two hours and a lifetime later, the doctor pops in. His eyes hold deep unease. My mother grabs my hand, and my father holds hers. I brace myself for what's to come, Naomi standing at my side, looking strong enough to handle what may come our way.

"So, we discovered that you have stage two pancreatic cancer, and we need to start treatment immediately to keep it from spreading to other portions of your body. Treatment will be aggressive, but we believe that it will cure you if we get a jump on it now."

I look around the room at my family. It's clear we're all thinking the same thing. When I told my parents about the pregnancy, they were just as excited as me. I didn't think I'd need to be worried about the possibility of having cancer, none of us did.

"And the baby? How will this affect my child?"

"My advice is always in the preservation of life, but if you continue your pregnancy, your baby won't make it through treatment. If you avoid treatment, you and your baby could both die from the cancer."

The breath feels like it's been snatched right out of my lungs.

"Are you saying I have to abort my baby?" My voice is shrill and full of shock.

"It's your choice, Grace, but those are the options I have to offer. I don't mean to sound so rash, but, Grace, you don't have much time to decide. You'll need to make a decision soon. I'll give you and your family some time. Please have the nurse page me should you need anything."

Doctor Cohen leaves his words lingering behind like he

didn't just ruin my life with a few sentences. When he's gone, I look up at Naomi. "Take me the hell home right now! I'm not staying here. I need to go home!"

Naomi shakes her head, like she isn't interested in doing that. "I think you should stay here and ask all the questions you need to ask. You have a lot of things to think about."

"Naomi, shut up! I've asked all the questions I want to ask. Please take me home!" I demand, my fists even bang the side of the bed.

Naomi shakes her head, but for now, I don't care. This feels just as bad as when I lost Noah. Noah…That's when it hit me. I need to get home so I can discuss this with him. He's the only person that can give me an answer to the question I seek. He's the only one who can say something right now that will mean anything to me.

"Please, Mom, take me home. I need to go home."

"Ok, shhh, baby. We'll take you home. Me and your father. We can talk about this more once things calm down."

I agree and stand up. "I'm going to put my clothes on and then we can go. Thanks Mom."

She smiles, though I know it isn't genuine. They think I'm crazy, that my behavior is insane, but they don't understand how it feels, how I'm feeling. I look over at Naomi, knowing I need to apologize, but I can't right now. I need some space to figure things out. My parents leave the room, and I'm able to put my clothes back on in peace. Naomi stays but only to make sure I can put my clothes on correctly.

"I know you're hurting right now, and I want to be by your side. I love you, you're like my sister."

I shake my head at Naomi. "I get it. I love you, too, but I

know where you will stand. We've had this conversation before in a hypothetical situation. I don't want anyone choosing me over my baby. I need to be able to make my own decision. This is my life, and I haven't asked for anyone else's opinion, yet everyone thinks they should give it to me, even by just suggestively making eye gestures and their body language."

Naomi places her hand on my shoulder in a loving manner. I know what she's feeling, and I understand why she's so upset and worried, but she has to trust that I'll make the best decision. Naomi helps me to finish getting ready so that I can ride home with my parents. I'll talk to Naomi again; this isn't the end for us. I just need space to make my own choice for now.

Stumbling into the house, I rush straight for the bedroom and slam the door where Noah is in his usual place, on the bed waiting for me. Seeing his face brings a sense of anger over me. I couldn't wait to get home to him, but now that I have something major comes to mind that I can't unthink. I sit at the edge of the bed, thinking. His reappearance didn't happen until after I got sick again. I've asked him repeatedly why and how he was back here with me and he continues to say he's here for me. The more my mind processes the words "I'm here for you" I quickly realize that he could have meant it in a different context. Meaning, he's physically here for me. My heartrate goes from zero to one hundred as the thoughts that are circulating through my mind right now aren't pleasant.

I turn around, snapping my head in his direction. His face says it all. His expression is an admission of guilt.

"You knew, didn't you?" I interrogate him, standing to my feet. I don't care that my parents are downstairs or that they might hear me. I need to get this out. I rush over to his side. His head is drooping downward, he can't look me in the eyes.

Pushing him, I shout again. "You knew? This is your fault! You could've told me I was carrying your baby, that I was sick and needed help! Why didn't you tell me?"

My knees feel weak as I drop to the bed, my head instinctively falls onto his chest.

"I...I tried to tell you, but I didn't have the heart to break the bad news to you, baby. You wouldn't have believed me anyway. You wouldn't have listened," he whispers, his words calming me as he places his arm around my shoulder and plants sweet kisses along the edge of my hairline.

I finally calm myself, trying to understand what's next. I made such a big deal with Naomi about how I feel and what I want, but I haven't really given it enough thought. What should I do? If I abort the baby, I could possibly save my life by seeking treatment. If I opt out of treatment and continue with the pregnancy, I would be endangering both of our lives. A third option would be to abort my baby and kill myself as well. Looking at Noah, he feels guilty enough, and I need to think for the both of us. I have so much to think about and imminent decisions to make. I don't have the pleasure of pouting. My life, and the life of my unborn child, depend on me being strong.

When I'm calm enough, I walk around to the other side of the bed and get comfortable. Noah leans back on the bed and relaxes as well.

"I'm not mad at you, I just need some time to process." I look into his eyes, and it seems as though he understands.

"So, we're having a baby?" he grins childishly.

His laughter becomes infectious, breaking the tension in the air. "Yeah, we are," I inform him.

His eyes light up, but as quickly as they light up the happiness fades into sadness.

"What's wrong?" I sit up, directing my attention to him.

Our hands collapsed onto one another in embrace, "I've always wanted nothing more than to start a life with you, a family. And I did. And now we're having out first child, only I can't help. I can't do any fucking thing because I'm dead, I'm gone. This child will never know me. I'll never be present, only the man from the pictures you tell them about. I'll never be able to leave my imprint on their life."

Noah's confession of his internal thoughts sends chills down my spine. All this time I'd only thought about what I was going to do regarding the pregnancy and treatment, I haven't had time to consider how Noah feels about anything.

"Noah, honey, I'm so sorry. I hadn't thought about things from that aspect. This makes things even more difficult."

"Me voicing how I feel was not intended to make things more difficult for you. I know I'm dead, I know why I was returned to you, but that still doesn't make it easy for me. Having a chance to come back is somewhat like torture because I know my staying won't be permanent. I'll eventually have to move on. I can't stay here with you in this form."

Avoiding a crying spell, Noah's jawline flexes and he pulls me closer. I can literally feel the pain, the hurt, he's experiencing right now. I snuggle up to him, my head on his chest.

He starts with forehead kisses and that transitions into something more.

"Noah…" I speak, barely above a whisper as he trails his fingertips along the inner part of my right thigh.

"Let me."

I relax my body and give in to the intense sexual sensation coursing through my system.

"I can't do much else for you right now. I can't provide, I can't stay for long, but I can pleasure you into oblivion. Let me make love to you, let me make you feel good. I promise you I won't disappoint you."

"You say you don't provide as if you've never done anything for me before. You were everything and then some to me. You're the one who helped me get on the right track. Don't say that, it's not true."

"I know, baby, but considering current circumstances, I'm sure you understand what I mean."

"I do," I admit, wanting to ensure he knows that his return to me is not helpless or unwanted.

As we now have a baby in tow, Noah carefully shifts me onto my back, spreading my thighs. He positions himself between my thighs and just smiles down at me.

"I know you may not be in the mood for any physical contact, so tonight I just want you to lay back and relax. Give me permission to pleasure you tonight."

Unable to utter a word, I just nod.

I lay my head back, eyes to the ceiling, as he removes my clothing. Once I'm completely undressed, Noah starts by spreading my thighs North and South. Mounting my calves over his shoulders, he lays chest down on the bed with his face only inches away from my honey pot. The thought of what he's going to do to me arouses me within a matter of seconds, but the thought of his actions is nothing compared to what he does.

Using the index and middle fingers on his right hand, he parts my labia and smooches my clitoris. My body reacts instantaneously, sending a wave of goosebumps over me. Not sparing a moment, Noah's tongue adorns the tip of my clit and the magic begins. I'm instantly taken, left speechless, as his tongue flicks briskly. As a means of holding my composure, I grip a handful of the comforter, pulling it upward toward me, making a complete mess of the bed. I believe my reaction only fuels him because the stance of his tongue widens over my pussy, taking it all into his mouth. The slurping sounds are only a bonus and pull me into a trance as he works on me. I begin to twirl my pussy around in his face, begging him to take all of me, to take my soul. He takes the hint and inserts the middle finger of his left hand into my canal, toying with my g-spot, but never pulls his tongue away from my center. I attempt to clamp my thighs shut but he overpowers me. He pulls me downward and continues to work on me. The pressure builds until I can't hold it anymore. The sexual tensions breaks, releasing, flowing outward in the form of creamy, sticky white cum. Noah wastes nothing, he cleans me up in one slurp. I look down between my legs to find him staring at me, beard soaked in my juices.

After two weeks, I've returned to the doctor once more for a checkup. And I'm not alone. My parent's and Naomi are by my side.

"Today, we can find out the sex of your baby, if he or she is positioned properly during the ultrasound," the technician informs us. Everyone in the room looks unhappy, but I've made my decision. I'm at peace.

"I'm actually going to wait until the baby is born. I want the sex of the baby to be a surprise."

An odd silence fills the room. It's obvious they don't agree with my decision.

The doctor comes in, and he overhears what I've said. I can tell by the look on his face he's not happy with my decision.

"I just want to reiterate that you may not make it to term, and that not seeking treatment could kill you and your child."

I smirk and combat him with the only thing higher than a doctor's opinion.

"I have faith that God will see me through. He hasn't brought me this far to leave me. Now, if we can get to the ultrasound..." I move my hand in a motion that says I'm ready to move forward.

After my appointment, I'm left with a sense of pride in the fact I stood up for myself. Voicing myself is the best thing I could have done because ultimately this is my body, my baby, and my decision. Today's the first time I've been able to drive myself to the doctor, so to say I'm excited is surely an understatement.

I prance to the car with confidence, knowing I've done what's right for me. Sliding into the car, I put my seatbelt on and start the car. When I look up into my rearview mirror, Noah appears in the backseat. I smile, excited to see him. I haven't even shared with him what I'm doing. The engine turns over, and I put my foot, my destination set for home.

"What did you decide, baby?" He has his arms folded across his chest with a smile.

"I decided to keep the baby and I'm going to turn down treatment," I answer in a matter-of-fact tone.

"Mmm...you sure that's what you want to do?" The inquisition in his tone makes me feel a bit uncomfortable.

"I'm positive. Our baby deserves a chance at life. This baby is your legacy, our legacy. I have faith, and I need you to have it too. God isn't through with us yet. I want to see it through until the baby is born. Tell God to give me a few more months. I'm not going to lose this baby."

"Baby, you can have children any time. You can't risk your life like this…."

"I can, and I will, but I don't think I'm risking anything. Trust the process. Trust God, we're going to be ok."

Before either of us can say another word, the passenger side door opens, and Naomi gets into the car, followed by my parents who slip into the back seat. I look for him in the rearview once more and Noah's gone. Maybe he went to relay my message.

EIGHT

I'd be a liar to say that as the time goes by, I'm happy. Every day, something hurts. Simply put, I don't feel well. I'm not physically well, but it's all worth it when I see my belly growing, even if it's not as much progress as the doctor would like.

Hours have turned into days, days into weeks, and weeks into months. On my bad days, and I have many of them, I'm happy to have Noah by my side. He comforts me in more ways than I can express. We've opted out of having sex through penetration and have opted for oral sex. It's safer and less taxing on my body.

I'm seven months pregnant now, and as my husband and caregiver, Noah is doing everything he can to be supportive. He hasn't missed a beat. Doctor Cohen has repetitiously recommended ending my pregnancy, but my child already had fingers and toes the first time I went to the doctor. There was no way after seeing an actual child inside of me I could terminate, regardless of the circumstances. I get rid of it, no matter the circumstances.

Doctor Cohen offers the option to receive a less strenuous treatment option but because my condition has weakened doing so isn't a good idea. Fortunate for me one of my classmates is a resident at a hospital not far away from home. This doctor is the top PEDS surgeon in the United States and has basically promised me they can remove the baby early, in a healthy state, so that I can seek treatment as quickly as possible. Hopefully, as Dr. Cohen has mentioned, it's not too late.

Today I have surgery. It's something I've been preparing for, for weeks. I've been with Noah every as often as I can. Before going under the knife, I feel the need to square things away with him, to ask him to talk to God on my behalf. I want nothing more than for me and the baby to make it through this alive and intact.

In a hospital gown, I lay nervously, nervously waiting to be wheeled off to surgery.

Somehow, he's manifested himself into the hospital today.

"I love you. Will you be here when I get back?" I break the silence between us once we're left alone to communicate.

"Always for you, my love. I'll be here." He strokes my high cheekbones.

With him endorsement, I now feel comfortable and safe to go into surgery.

Interrupting us, Naomi enters the room.

"I need to talk to you, Grace, and it's about something important."

I sit up in my bed, propping myself. A part of me is hoping

we can reconcile, especially because I don't know where we're going with this conversation.

"I can't get something out of my head, and I need to address it, immediately."

"Oh God, here we go. Is this about Noah again?" I cut my eyes at her, folding my arms across my chest.

"You know it is. I don't think it's healthy for you to keep this up, and I can't let you go under the knife without saying it. I don't know what's going to happen, but when you come back, I need you to get it together. You're acting like a crazy person, Grace. Noah is dead!"

"You know what your problem is, Naomi? You're lonely, and you have nothing better to do than make me miserable. Am I not struggling enough, going through enough?"

The monitor that's keeping track of my blood pressure starts beeping faster and faster. My heartrate was steady before the conversation ensued. "It isn't Noah that's making my condition worse; it's you!"

Naomi's eyes shift back and forth between me and the monitor, my eyes are doing the same.

"Ok, calm down. We don't have to talk about this right now. I'm sorry, I didn't mean to—"

"Oh, yes you did. You did mean to upset me. Noah has been with me the entire step of the way. God, why can't you just let me live?"

"O-ok, Grace. I'm sorry, just calm down."

I barely hear her words. Everything in my mind sounds like I'm under water, drowning. My chest hurts, and I feel sharp pains passing through my stomach. The doctors rush in, I'm seconds away from closing my eyes.

"Grace, Grace, can you hear me? We need a crash cart stat!"

I'm barely here with everyone else. "She needs to get to the OR NOW!" Dr. Cohen shouts over me.

Naomi takes a few steps back, her hand covering her mouth. I'm rushed to the OR me back to the OR. Everything's happening so fast that I can't keep up.

"Grace, right now we can't worry about removing any parts of the tumor. With her heartrate up and the baby showing to be in distress, we'll need to safely deliver the baby and get you stabilized before we can do anything else. Just relax for me, breathe."

I follow his instruction, allowing my body to relax as I'm pumped with meds so that surgery can begin. A million thoughts are running through my mind as I feel the medication taking over my speech, sight, and motor skills. I just want a healthy baby.

I wake feeling empty, lighter. Opening my eyes, I find myself in an all-white room with a white slip on. I peer around, and I see a figure walking toward me. As it moves closer, I realize it's Noah. He's smiling at me. With his hand out, he takes mine, helping me sit up. Face to face, he kisses me but something seems off. The energy isn't quite right.

I glance at Noah once more and tears are flowing like a raging river.

"Oh, honey! What's wrong? Are you hurt?" I begin searching his body over, looking for anything that could be giving him pain.

"Baby, you have to fight. Now, more than ever, I need you to be

strong. Our son needs you, baby. He won't make it in this world without you..."

"S-son? Oh my God, am I dead? What's happening?" I start to panic, but as always, Noah is the calm to my storm.

"You're dying, yes, but you can go back. You have to fight to get back in time, and yes...a son. A beautiful son. Please, fight, so you can have a lifetime with our son."

Noah kisses my hands, begging me to do what I can to get back to our son. My heart strings pull, once, twice, three times. On the third pull, I'm catapulted back into my body, just as I hear Doctor Cohen calling my time of death.

I take a deep gasp of air.

"Her heart is beating on its own! Let's get stabilized!" the doctor announces, and his team get to work. I haven't opened my eyes, but I can hear everything. I can hear the nurses moving around the room in their respective spots to make sure I'm ok, to do what needs to be done to save my life.

Once my body is stable, my eyes shoot open. I'm remembering the most important thing—my son.

"W-where's my son?" I ask, my throat feeling like razor blades, it's so dry.

"How did you know he's a boy, Grace?" Doctor Cohen asks.

I smile in return as only a part of my response. "My husband told me."

NINE

$\mathcal{A}$fter several hours of being in a recovery room, the only thing I want is to spend time with my son, to see his face. I barely saw him before they took him, and he is the only thing I can think of. I've requested to see him so many times, I feel like nobody's listening to me. I'm about to hit the help button for the fifteenth time when a doctor comes in, followed by Naomi. My parents decided to go for food and get a few things so they'd be comfortable at the hospital with me.

"Hi, Grace. That baby boy of yours is an absolute looker." Doctor Cohen smiles, nodding his head.

"Thank you. I wish I could say that myself, but no one will bring me my baby. Where is he?"

I look behind the doctor, hoping the door will fling itself open, and my baby will be there, but it doesn't happen.

"I know you're eager to see your little one, and you will just as soon as I finish going over a few things with you. Now, your tumor is locally advanced, so me and my team are recommending aggressive chemo and radiation before the surgery can be performed."

"Fine, do whatever we need to do. I just want to see my baby." My arms are folded over my chest. The only thing I care about is seeing my baby.

"I'll let the nurse know you're ready to see him, and I'll see what I can do about getting your surgery ready."

I nod. Hopefully the doctor was serious about bringing me my baby. I gave birth hours ago. Silence fills the room as I wait for them to bring the baby. But I'm dying to tell somebody, anybody who will listen that I knew I was having a son before I even woke up. I don't care if Naomi gets mad or not; I have to tell her.

"Naomi, you wanna hear something crazy but true?"

She looks up from her seat, staring me directly in the face. "Sure, what's up?"

"I knew he was a boy." If I could get up and move around I would. I'm practically bouncing up and down in the hospital bed.

"How? Did you see his penis on the ultrasound beforehand?"

It seems like now I have her full attention, and her eyebrows are raised in a dubious manner.

"No, Noah told me. When I flatlined...I saw him. He was—"

"Enough, Grace!" Naomi exclaims as she slams her purse on the table. "God, I've had enough of this Noah crap. You have to get it together. You have a son to raise now. You have to get better!"

"Better? I'm not sick in the mind. I promise you, Noah is real, and he's here right now!" I beat my fists against my blanket.

"That's it. I'm going to tell them you need psychiatric care. This has gone so far, and I've tried to ask you to stop, to get you to realize you're crazy, and your condition is worse because of it, but you just won't listen!"

I shake my head and look over at Noah. "Can I show her? She doesn't believe me, and I can't keep hiding you. I'm glad you showed up when you did."

I lift my hand and hold it in his. Noah's eyes are kind and gentle. He's so understanding.

"You've got to be kidding me. You're talking to yourself!"

"Sit down, just trust me. Just watch. Please, trust me. Give me a chance to show you."

Naomi's face is twisted in confusion, but I can tell she knows I believe this, and I'm serious, so she takes a seat and keeps staring at me.

"Just open your mind to what I'm saying. Close your eyes."

Naomi takes a deep breath and pushes it out. She then places her hands in her lap, and her face straightens once more. Naomi nods her head when she's ready.

Noah strolls across the room. His movements are always precise, but so effortless; he looks like he's floating. He makes it to Naomi's side and bends down. He's on the ball of his feet, and he reaches up, resting his hand on Naomi's shoulder.

"Uhhhh!" she gasps. I realize she can feel it. "What the hell?" she asks, more so questioning herself about what she felt rather than about if it happened or not. Noah smiles and rises back to his feet and then leans over Naomi.

"I can feel his breath on my forehead…." She acknowledges, a smile popping up on her face. Noah kisses her on the right corner of her forehead.

"Oh my God...Grace," her words come in as a whisper. She can't believe what she's just experienced. "Grace...I'm so sorry for ever doubting you, and you too, Noah, wherever you might be."

Tears flood Naomi's eyes. She's elated to know Noah is here with us. Now she understands what I've been experiencing, that I'm not crazy, that Noah has been with me throughout this process.

An awkward silence takes over, as Naomi is still in shock of this revelation.

Mom and Dad enter, breaking our silence, with smiles on their faces.

"Hi, sweetheart, how are you feeling?" Mom starts first, taking a seat on the left side of the bed, now holding my hand.

"I'm doing good. I have some news, by the way," I announce. Everyone in the room stops moving. I feel bad. Now because of my condition, any time I say I have something to say or want to talk about, things get still. They're afraid of what I will say.

"Everyone can rest easy. I just wanted you guys to know I've decided to name the baby after Noah. Noah Junior."

"Oh, honey that's a fine thing to do. Fine indeed," Dad responds. I can tell he really is pleased, though I know he would've preferred I name my son after him.

Mom and Naomi congratulate me, and I feel like the best is yet to come. It's all I can hope for now that I've got my baby boy and Noah. I can have both, and I can be happy.

Six Months Later

"I can't help myself. I love you and nobody else. Duhn-duhn-duhn-duhn..." I sing to Noah Jr.

He likes to hear my voice, and it keeps us both calm when I sing. My baby boy came into the world a little earlier than expected, but he's healthy and strong. Our favorite time together is when we're singing and dancing. It's our own little thing, that is until his look-a-like of a father appears.

"Noah, not that I'm not happy to see you, but you've been here a lot. Are you sure everything's ok?"

I've been asking him this question nearly every day. Before, he only appeared every so often, but since I've come home with the baby and started taking my treatments, he's here all the time. My parents have been here too. And, of course, Naomi. They're too afraid to leave me completely alone with the baby because my condition seems to be deteriorating, as much as I hate to admit it. My cancer has grown to stage three and is progressing like wildfire.

"Isn't it enough that I want to spend time with you and our son, my love? I miss you deeply when I'm not here. I just want to make sure you're not getting overwhelmed."

I'm bouncing Noah Jr. in my arms as I sweep my body around to face Noah. Something about what he's saying doesn't add up. I can hear the undertone of something being wrong. It's what he's *not* saying that scares me.

"Overwhelmed? No, that's not it. Tell me," I search his eyes for truth. I don't know why he won't be open with me. Maybe he thinks I'm too fragile. Whatever the case may be, I need his honest more than anything in this moment.

A thought crosses my mind and I panic, "Oh my God, am I going to die? Are you trying to warn me? Are you giving me time with N.J. before it's time? Oh, God, please!" I cry out, panting. I can't take one more hit. I can't lose my son, and he can't lose me, not yet.

"No, baby. You're not going to die. I really want to spend time with you and the baby."

I decide not to let Noah bother me. I have no choice but to believe him. I know him better than anyone, and I know he's lying. While NJ and I dance around the room, something inside of me changes drastically. The energy I just had seems to be fleeting. This is the most energy I've had in weeks. I normally have to hold NJ in the bed, but today, I've been able to rock him and dance with him around the house, no issues.

"Hey, Pumpkin. Would you like a grilled cheese for lunch?" I hear my father's voice, and I try to turn around to answer him, but my body doesn't respond. I feel as if I've gone numb. I can't feel my legs or my hands. One minute, I'm holding NJ and the next he's tumbling out of my hands; we're both falling. Before I collapse, NJ is caught. My eyes begin to roll backwards as my head bounces from the floor. Everything goes dark and I feel myself slipping into unconsciousness.

TEN

September 2019 – Wedding Day

"Wise men say, only fools rush in...
But I can't help...
Falling in love with you...."

"*M*ay I have this dance, Mrs. Richardson?" Noah bows to me, his hand outstretched in my direction. *My feet are killing me, but for him, I can muster up the energy to keep going.*

"You may, Mr. Richardson." I give him my hand in response.

He helps me to my feet and leads me to the middle of the dance floor. My ivory hued lace dress flows freely behind me. Our guests clear the dancefloor as we approach. As we take our stance and prepare for our first dance as Mr. and Mrs. Richardson, the crowd is awing at the sight of us. The DJ plays the perfect song to start the reception off right.

"I can't wait to spend the rest of my life with you, Noah. We'll have kids, great careers, a special—"

"Shh...I don't need or want all that. You're all I've ever wanted, and now that I have you, my life is complete. A baby would be nice, three, to be exact, but as long as I have you, I'm fulfilled. You are my everything. There is no me without you," he reassures me.

I nestle my head on his chest, as he his hands on my hips. I can't think of anything else that can top this admittance of love. Today, my wedding day, has been perfect. I could have married Noah in a shack, and, still, I'd be happy. We took those vows today, to love, honor, cherish, and protect one another through sickness and health. I plan to keep that promise, and I know he will too. He's my dream, and it's finally come true.

I finally come to but I'm having an outer body experience. I'm freely floating above my body, able to view everyone in the OR.

"Oh God, NJ? Where's my baby?" I speak, but I realize no one can hear me.

I gauge my surroundings and realize I'm in the hospital. Doctors are encircling me, nurses rushing around the room. The doctors rotate my bed and run like hell toward the OR. After months of treatment, the doctors feel confident they might be able to remove the tumor and continue chemo and radiation, as necessary.

Every time I get comfortable in this life, something tries to take me away again, but I won't let it.

With the first incision, I'm alert; my outer body is alert. I have to know how this will turn out, and I can only hope for the best.

"Do you see this? Look," Doctor Cohen says, he's moving his instruments inside of me.

"The tumor has shrunk significantly. It looks like we're back in phase two ladies and gentlemen," he speaks, a deep sigh of relief escaping him.

This is the best damn news I've heard since the birth of NJ. I'm going to live! I will see Noah again. Before I become one with my body once more, I overhear Dr. Cohen saying they've removed eighty percent of the mass, and I can go to recovery, that I did well.

A few hours later, I wake to the sound of my mother praying. I smile at the sentiment, but as always, my priority is my son. I look around the room for him, and I've caught my mother's attention.

"Oh, sweetheart, welcome back. You scared us." My mother squeezes my hand gently.

"We should be used to this by now. Where's NJ?" I look around her to check my dad. NJ's nowhere to be found.

"He's with Naomi. Being that he was born prematurely and he's doing well, we wanted to make sure that that remains the case. We didn't want to put him at risk by bringing him up here, so Naomi is taking care of him."

I want to protest the decision they've made but deep down I know it's in his best interest. I don't get a chance to speak before Dr. Cohen graces us with his presence.

"Hello, again, Grace. We've got some great news…"

This is news I already have, considering I saw it firsthand myself, but I will humor the doctor.

"What is it?"

"Most of the tumor was removed during surgery. Once we opened you up, we noticed the tumor had shrunk significantly. With that said, I think we should get more aggressive and do a few more rounds of chemo and radiation. This will ensure the tumor is gone completely, with no possibility of growing back. I'd like to get you set up and on a new schedule…"

"Doctor, with all due respect," I interrupt him respectfully. "I'm not doing another moment of chemo or radiation, and I mean that. I'm simply not doing it again." I shrug my shoulders, sticking to my decision.

I watch each facial expression in the room go from happy, to shock, to worry. It's obvious they didn't expect this response.

"I can't lie, Grace. I am a bit shocked to hear this. I mean, chemo and radiation are what helped to shrink your tumor, without it—"

"Without it, I'll be just fine. Listen, Doctor, Mom and Dad, I am blessed and highly favored by God. I've been on the other side of light more times than anyone in this room, so I think I'm starting to get that God's plan is a long game for me, not a short one. What I do know is my body nor my spirit can take another ounce of treatment. If I'm going to leave this earth, I want to spend time with my son. Most of the time, I'm too weak to hold him, and when I do, it's so fast. At times, I don't feel like a real mother. He'll be walking and talking before we know it, and I don't want to miss it because of "treatment" that makes me feel like shit."

It feels so good to get that off my chest. I've tried saying it a million times, but every time I try, it just seems to upset everyone. Through all of this, I've come to realize I can't worry about how everyone else feels. It's imperative I worry about myself first.

Dad walks closer to the bed, and he rests his hands on the guard rails. "Sweetheart, we have no choice but to respect you and your wishes, but if you change your mind, we can always get started. That's not me just saying that. I, well, we, will respect your wishes, no matter what they are."

I smile at my dad and look over to the doctor. He now seems to be on board with how I'm feeling, and I'm glad we're all on the same page.

"Great, now what's a girl gotta do to get discharged? I miss being around my son, and I'm eager to get home!"

I can't believe I'm finally at home! I was only gone about three days, but that was three days too long. Naomi still has NJ, but now that I'm home, she'll be returning him. While I wait, I decide to take a shower. Doing everything now will ensure I get the maximum time with NJ.

This is the first time in months I've had the energy to shower on my own, and I'm going to take pride in doing it, since it's been so long. When I enter the bathroom, I shut the door, my floor length mirror reveals my naked body.

I take an exasperated breath. I haven't seen myself completely naked for some time. I didn't know my illness had physically consumed me. My collar bones are sharp and pointed like a witch. I've lost so much of my happy and natural weight, I'm practically skin and bones now. No wonder my family has been worried about me; they probably think I'm seconds away from death at all times.

For the few minutes I'm feeling bad for myself, I suddenly feel loving arms around my waist; Noah's with me. His smile is genuine and strong, not forced. He appears to be happy to see me.

"I still think you're the most beautiful woman in the world. Your body is a demonstration of your ability to push through. You're a survivor. You're a strong woman of God, and I know you'll pull through this if you cling to your faith."

Noah kisses my neck as we stare into the mirror, gazing at one another. His embrace is as warm as it's always been. I know he wants me to pray, he wants me to start clinging to my faith now, not later, but right now. I begin speaking once more.

"Dear Heavenly Father, I come humbly but boldly to your throne. You said where two or more are gathered in your name, it shall be done. I come to you in fellowship, along with my husband, to thank you Lord. I want to thank you for your grace and mercy, for your honor and blessings, God. To thank you for sparing me, for sparing my son, for loving me enough to continue giving me life."

My eyes are wet as I cry out to the lord, thanking him for all he's done. "I thank you, for a support system, God. For a beautiful son, for his health, for my continued life, God. I ask that you continue to see me through this journey called life, God. I ask that you continue to help me fulfill my purpose, so that I might live and not die. I believe in your word, Lord. I know you will not leave nor forsake me, God. I've never seen the righteous fall, Lord, and I won't see it today, God. I know I won't. Continue to pour into me, Father, as I continue to worship you through the good and the bad, Lord. For your many blessings, you deserve all the praise, all the honor, and all the glory. In your son Jesus Christ's name, amen!"

"Amen," Noah and I say simultaneously.

I feel power like I've never felt before surging through me. The power of God has a hold on me, and I'm more than confident that he will continue to show me favor.

Noah wipes the tears from my eyes and kisses me with intent. I take in his love and step to the side to get into the shower. I just want to wash the feeling of being in the hospital off me. Within a few minutes, Noah washes me from head to toe and helps me out the shower and into comfortable clothing. Noah oils my body down, massaging every inch of me until I fall prey to the sandman.

ELEVEN

My health has improved greatly and I'm getting stronger by the day. Today's my first day back at work in what seems like an eternity. I sit in the parking lot, contemplating on making the first move to head toward the building. I've been sitting here for at least thirty minutes, just staring at the building. I have to make a move. I close my eyes and pray once more then head for the building.

Determined not to let the day get to me, I brave the walk through the building to the elevators. The elevator dings and when it opens, I let out a sigh of relief. I'm fortunate to find the elevator unoccupied.

After climbing several floors to reach my destination, the elevator doors open, and the floor is as busy as it's always been. I glide through, unnoticed. Using my key, I unlock my office and let myself in. The room is stuffy and smells stale. My desk is exactly as I left it, with post it notes and files all over it.

To the left of my office, normally Liana is at her desk, taking calls, running around the office like a chicken with her head cut off. She'd usually be here to greet me.

I make myself comfortable in my chair and begin sifting through the paperwork mon my desk. My mind goes haywire as I look at everything before me. It's as if nothing was done in my absence. I toss the paperwork to the side momentarily and log into my computer, checking for emails. Hopefully, the emails will give me some indication of what I've missed.

"Seven hundred and sixty unread emails? My God!?" I exclaim.

I can feel the anxiety rising in my veins thinking about going through all these messages, and I know there's no way I'll get through them all. Not today, at least. The best thing I can do at this point is enlist some help.

Picking up my phone, I'm just about to hit the button that reads "assistants" when my office door bursts open unannounced. Yvonne is rushing toward me like a torpedo.

"Good morning, Yvonne."

"Morning, Grace. I assume that we can expect to see you every day?" she asks, tilting her glasses, glancing over at me.

"Yes ma'am. I plan on it. It seems like I'm extremely behind though. I was just about to call one of the assistants in here to catch me up."

Yvonne nods and then looks down at my desk.

"Yes, well, I'll leave you to it. I just wanted to come in and greet you. I won't be available for most of the day, so I wanted to do it while there was still time."

"Thank you. Before you go, where is Liana? She normally handles all the logistics and things for me. Her desk looks bare."

"Yes, that's because Liana is no longer an assistant. She was promoted several months ago. You can find her on the eighth floor now."

Yvonne turns around and rushes out of the door, sucking the air right out of my body. Liana is on the eighth floor now which means she's surpassed me. I'm happy for her, but that just means things really have changed.

Now that Yvonne is gone, I finish making the phone call I previously started and call an assistant to my office. Thirty seconds tick by before a lanky woman appears in my doorway with an iPad in her hands.

"Good morning, Grace. You called?"

"Yes, come in and have a seat," I greet her. "I was hoping you could catch me up. I've been gone for quite some time."

She nods her head and takes a seat on the other side of my desk and crosses her legs as she leans forward.

"Alright, we've completely upgraded our system for customers. I'll show you."

"What is your name, by the way?" I ask, trying to create some rapport between us.

"It's Angie. I was a temp before you left, and now I have a permanent position."

I nod. She taps a series of things on her iPad and then presents what she sees to me.

"As you can see here, everything is color coordinated. Red means the clients have scheduled appointments, yellow means the clients need to schedule an appointment, and green means their appointment is today or within 24 hours. Your client list has been taken over by Josh, but I'm sure they'll be happy to have you back. Now, I know you specialize in the e-commerce side of things, so you take care of our web design, virtual clients, and all that. If you look over here, this is a spreadsheet of clients you need to contact who have submitted an online form for more information..."

The more Angie speaks, I find myself more lost than I was before she arrived. It's evident that things have evolved around the office and I feel as if I've just stepped out of the Jurassic period. For the next thirty minutes, Angie continues about the new computer systems, how to reach my clients versus the old way, and more importantly, how my desk phone will be changed out as of today.

"And then—"

"You know what, Angie? I'm sorry I've made you waste your time. This was a huge mistake." I stand firmly and gather the things I brought in with me.

"But Grace, wh-what are you doing?"

Chuckling, I throw my head back. "I'm quitting. I know this makes no sense to you, and I'm sure you're wondering why I even came in if I was just going to quit. Well, I didn't know I was going to quit, but I am. This isn't the place for me anymore. It doesn't feel the same. Liana isn't down here. I came back to get some normalcy, and this is far from my norm. You did a great job explaining yourself, but I'm done with this."

There's something about what I just said to Angie that brings me an overwhelming sense of liberation. Her mouth is hanging wide open in disbelief as I work to gather my things.

"W-was it something I said? Did I not explain something thoroughly enough?"

"Oh, no, Angie, this has nothing to do with you at all. This is something that I need to do. I'll talk with Yvonne before I leave. Thank you, Angie, and the best of luck to you on your journey here with the company. This is a promising company, especially if you're looking to climb the ladder or even retire in the coming years."

"I can have Yvonne come to you if you'd like. She's not due to her next meeting for another 10 minutes," Angie offers.

"That would be great. I'll finish gathering my things." She nods and disappears beyond my office door.

While I wait for Yvonne, I remove my badge, remove all work-related keys from my keyring, and lay out my company cell phone and laptop for return. Once I have those things in order, I take a spare box from the closet in my office and begin to pack my personal belongings, including the photo of Noah and I that I dropped and shattered the last time I was here at work. This moment is bittersweet, but I truly believe I'm being led away from this and toward something more suited for my new lifestyle.

"So, I hear you're wanting to leave me permanently?" Yvonne emerges, her body propped against the door frame.

"Yeah, I'm so sorry I came in today and wasted everyone's time. I just don't feel as though I have a place here anymore..." I begin to explain. Yvonne interrupts.

"No need to explain, Grace. I don't know what you've experienced or how you're feeling now, but your satisfaction in quitting is written all over your face. I see a sense of reprieve in you that I haven't seen since the passing of your husband. If anything, I'm congratulating you for taking this step, for doing what's best for you."

It takes nearly another hour, but I finalize everything at work and I'm escorted to the parking lot by my original team members, including Liana. With shared hugs, kisses, and short stories about our times together, I finally say my goodbyes.

As I settle into my vehicle, I feel I can close this chapter of my life with a smile. I'm leaving because it's right for me. Not because my husband died, not because I'm ill, but because I've evolved, I've grown.

Besides, entrepreneurship is practically in my blood; it's imbedded in me. It's what I went to school for. I put an emphasis on studying e-commerce so I could work digitally, so I could eventually start my own home-based business. Thanks to the job I'm walking away from today, I now have the skillset needed to survive and thrive from an entrepreneurial aspect. And I have just the products and services in mind to get me started. I've been holding these ideas, my niche, for years. It's time I use it.

———

Pulling up at the lake house, the first thing I see is Naomi on the porch with NJ. Deciding to leave everything from work in the car, I take my purse and get out.

"Look, there's Mommy!" Naomi points NJ in my direction.

I can't get on the porch quick enough. I swoop my baby boy into my arms, suffocating him with kisses. I'm truly happy to be home.

"How was it? I didn't expect you back so soon." Naomi asks, reclining her position in the oversize lawn chair on the porch.

"It was…enlightening to say the least."

"Enlightening? Well heck, enlighten." She chuckles, but she won't when I tell her what I've done. I take a seat next to her, still holding Junior in my lap. I look directly at her. "I quit my job. I just straight up left."

Naomi's eyes scream panic but she says nothing; she continues listen. I begin to ramble on about what led me to quitting and when I stop to take a breath, Naomi speaks.

"I'm not gonna lie, I'm shocked. Are you sure this is a good time for you to quit your job? I mean, I know you have savings and money from Noah's passing, but what about long term? I'm not trying to be in your business, I just want to make sure that you're ok."

"I can understand that," I respond in a lower tone. Jr. is falling asleep. "But trust me, I've got a good head for business. I always have. Don't forget, it's also what I went to school for. I didn't get that focus in E-commerce to work for someone else for the rest of my life."

Naomi doesn't miss a beat.

"You know, I didn't think of that, Grace! You do have a knack for that type of thing. Some people are just meant for such things. See, me on the other hand, I need structure so I guess I'll forever be working for someone else," she admits, laughing.

We talk a bit longer and I realize I need to speak with my parents. I had Jr. off to Naomi. She's going to lay him down for a nap and then head home. I remain on the porch. With a deep breath in, I pull out my cell and call my mother's phone. To my surprise, she picks up.

"Hey, Mom. How are you?"

"I'm fine, baby, how are you? How was your first day back at work?" Through the phone, I hear sounds of something being poured.

"Mom, what are you doing?" I ask dubiously.

"Pouring myself a glass of wine, if that's alright with you headmaster." She giggles in sarcasm. I chuckle along with her.

"Sorry, Mom. I just heard something. I didn't know if you were becoming a midday coffee drinker or what."

"Midday? Please, who do you take me for? You know, coffee in the middle of the day makes people crazy. I've got enough to do without adding midday crazy lady to the list. Now, stop avoiding my questions. How was today?"

"Well, I quit. I gave it some thought and going back just isn't in the cards for me." I slowly work to explain everything to my mother, as I did with Naomi."

"Well about damn time! I've always pushed you so hard because I knew you were more than a body sitting behind a desk. You're better than that, smarter than that. I feel that's why you struggled some years back to find your footing. God knew the paths you were attempting to take weren't for you. He guided you right to where you are now. I have so much faith in you and believe that without a shadow of a doubt you can handle this, you can make it work for you."

I blush at my mother's words. It seems like it's been ages since we've been able to speak openly to one another in such a manner. Her understanding and agreeance in my decision only fuels me.

"Ok, so graphic design is on the table. I can design a website quickly. I'm also thinking about virtual assistance. I've always been good at helping people, but I can do it on my terms. VA's can make a substantial amount of money if they know what they're doing, and I do, especially with all the experience I have with E-Commerce. I think I can do something that will be fun for me and still make money."

"Well, I think you should. What do you need to do to get started? Can your father and I do anything to help?"

Knowing Mom is just what I need to power through, to get things started.

"No, I can manage. If anything, spend some time with Noah while I get things up and running. I know I have some things to figure out and people to call in such a short timeframe. Having someone help with NJ would be appreciated."

"We'd be happy to see our grandson anytime. You just say the word and we'll be there."

"Thanks so much. You have no idea how much this means to me."

"Anytime baby. Anytime."

"Junior is taking a nap, and I think I'll have one with him. Care if we chat later?"

"Sure, but before you go, are you feeling ok?" Mom asks. I know she's referring to the cancer.

"I'm ok. I haven't had any bad bouts of pain, and I'm doing everything I can to stay healthy. I'm eating cleaner, getting my exercise in. I'm ok, just tired. Regular tired."

"Ok, good. You two get some rest. Call me later. I love you, Grace."

"Love you too, Mom."

———

It's been two months or so since I quit my job, and I know it was the right decision. Becoming a VA is a little more difficult than I formerly presumed. All the clients who kept reaching out to me after setting up a website were either way too demanding or didn't know exactly what they needed, so staying with graphic design for now has been a good idea.

So far, I've done over ten websites for multi-million-dollar companies, and if I can keep them on the roster for graphic design I'll be doing just fine. There are so many dreams and things floating around in my head, that I don't hear my name being called by the nurse. I forget I'm at the doctor's office.

"Grace are you ready?" she asks. I look up, finally snapping back to reality.

"Yes, I'm sorry."

"Follow me please."

Nurse Katherine leads to a private room where I await Dr. Cohen's appearance. I've come back for an ordinary checkup, as I have been for the last several weeks. I haven't told anyone that I've been coming in for checkups every two weeks. Today is no different, but it is the most important one for me thus far because NJ's first birthday is tomorrow. I want to assure I'm in the best shape possible for his big day.

A few minutes of almost chewing my fingernails off goes by, Dr. Cohen comes in. He stands in front of me, his clipboard in hand. He's looking at me, rocking back and forth. I'm practically holding my breath because I've never seen this reaction from him. As he begins to speak, I brace myself for anything.

NJ's First Birthday

"Sweetheart, you need to sit down. You're going to give yourself a panic attack," Mom says after noticing I'm on edge.

She pats me on the back, and then rubs my shoulder. I'm excited for Noah's birthday party, but also a little bit nervous. I just want everything to go well. I know he probably won't remember it, but there will be pictures. It seems like just yesterday Dr. Cohen was telling me it was better to abort my baby so that I could live, because having him could kill us both, but he's the healthiest baby. He doesn't have any of the problems. I've been blessed in so many ways, and I believe that may be attributing to my anxiety today.

"Go ahead and get ready. Your father and I will greet everyone as they arrive."

"Even Noah's parents, right?" I give Mom an 'I know how you like to act' look.

The people who raised Noah, God bless his soul, were much older when they adopted him. They passed away before he did. He was able to form a relationship with his biological parents as an adult, so I reached out to them, offering them an invite to today's festivities. They seemed to be please to meet their grandson, and I couldn't resist the thought of seeing Noah's biological family.

"We're just about set. Go ahead and get dressed. Naomi, your Dad, and I will add any final touches."

With Mom's permission, I run off to prepare myself for the party. I wash up, apply a fresh coat of makeup, and style my hair in a high messy bun. I add a wraparound dress, simple but elegant infinity necklace and large hoop earrings to complete the look.

I give myself one last look in the mirror before leaving the bathroom. This is the best I've seen myself in quite some time. My once frail body has now filled out nice and I'm back to the size I was around the time Noah and I reunited. Realizing I need to get going, I head for the door, hand on the knob, but there's something tugging at me. I feel like I'm missing something. And then it dawns on me.

"Noah," I breathe. I haven't seen him in quite some time.

"You look absolutely stunning honey," he whispers into my ear, delicately kissing me on the cheek.

"Thank you. I feel stunning. I feel...like myself." I smile wider than I mean to, and when I blink, he's gone, but I know he's close. I don't waste another second; I head downstairs for the party.

From the moment I open the door, I can hear the love being spread amongst the guests. Naomi surfaces, catching my attention, and she has a smile on her face. I can hear it in the influx in her voice. Naomi thrives at parties, so I know she's brought the best present for a baby. Mom, Dad, NJ, and Noah's parents are all gathered conversing, fighting for NJ's attention.

When I emerge, all eyes are on me. I see the deep breath everyone has taken.

"Is everything ok?" I question, giving everyone my full attention. Naomi's hands shoot up to her mouth.

"You look beautiful, Grace. Really."

I tilt my head with a kind smile. There's no better time than now to tell everyone the news I received yesterday during my appointment with Dr. Cohen.

"Thank you, Naomi, speaking of which. I have a bit of news to share with you about my condition."

Mom's eyes prickle with worry. I rush to her side and grab

her hand, giving her assurance that what I'm about to say will shock everyone.

"As most of you know, I decided against treatment after my surgery. I didn't care if it would take time to heal. I didn't care if it would take time for the tumor to shrink. I wasn't putting that on me or NJ, and I had faith that I would be ok. As of yesterday," I take a pause for dramatic effect and to stop myself from crying myself. "I'm in remission. The tumor has shrunk down to three percent, and the cancer cells are leaving my body."

Mom starts jumping up and down, and my father and Noah's both come over and hug me.

"We didn't even know you were sick, Grace," Noah's father says, his mustache partly going in his mouth when he speaks.

"I didn't tell anyone except these guys, and they wouldn't have even known had I not kept been so sick. Besides, it doesn't matter what happened before. All that matters is now I'm healthy, and I can dedicate all my attention and time to my son, the way I wanted, and the way God intended."

Noah's father lets go, and Naomi comes over, hugging me as tightly as a bear would.

"I'm so, so happy. I'm so proud of you. Oh God, now I'm trying not to cry."

Naomi fans herself so the tears don't fall. It must be contagious because I'm starting to feel the same.

"Everyone go ahead to the living room. I'm going to ice the cupcakes and I'll be in shortly," I say over my shoulder as I walk toward the kitchen.

NJ's on the floor playing with his blocks. Noah's father is playing alongside him. They may not have been able to make things right with Noah but I'm praying they stick around for

Junior. He's only met them today and he's already so fond of them. might not have been able to get it right with Noah, but I'm praying they stick around for Noah Junior, since he seems to be fond of them.

Thankfully, I made the icing last night, so all I have to do is lather it over the cupcakes. I Considering I'm crunched for time, I apply the icing to each cupcake, bringing them to a swirl in the middle. I discard the icing and reach for the cupcakes when my phone rings. Mom approaches as I answer the phone.

"Take there?" Mom mouths to me, careful not to disrupt my phone call.

I nod, giving her the thumbs up.

"Hello?" I answer, eager to get off the phone.

"Yes, is this Grace Middleton?" a woman's voice greets my ear. It's odd that she uses my maiden name. I haven't been called Grace Middleton in years.

"This is she. Who's calling?"

The phone is to my ear, and I can hear the words she's saying, but the words are like a punch to my gut. My throat is instantly dry, and I'm not sure of what to say. Nausea courses through my body, and I can feel I'm about to lose it. By the end of the phone call, I'm so shaken that I don't know what to do with the information I've been given. I keep reminding myself that today's about Noah. Nothing else matters today.

Snapping back into birthday mode, I grab the cupcakes and walk in singing, "Happy birthday to you, happy birthday to you, happy birthday dear Noah, happy birthday to you," I sing, leaving the phone call in the kitchen, and turning off that part of my brain for now.

TWELVE

My leg is filled with nervousness. It shakes uncontrollably as I wait anxiously for the receptionist to call my name. My stomach is literally in knots. I look around, and the words Stanton Fertility Cryobank are staring boldly at me. I've been here for about thirty-minutes, preparing myself for whatever news they have for me regarding Noah.

"Middleton," the receptionist calls.

The fact that she's calling me by my maiden name is, again, shocking. I assumed when they called before they were just verifying who I was without my married name. It happens, but now I'm wondering if that's truly the name they have on file for me, and why would they have that name instead of Richardson? Over the phone, I was told that I needed to come in so they could discuss closing out Noah's account. My thoughts are tangled trying to understand what kind of account he'd have here.

I follow the receptionist to a room where another lady awaits me.

"Hi, Grace, I'm Sylvia. I'm sorry it took so long for us to get in contact with you, but we're closing this location, and we're contacting those who donated their specimens to see if they'd like for us to discard the specimen or move it to the newest location."

"Specimen? You mean..."

"Yes, your husband, Noah Richardson, donated his semen, it looks like back in 2009." the receptionist says as she glances down over a stack of papers over her glasses.

"Really? Can I see?"

"Sure," she turns the paperwork around. "If you look right here, Noah listed you as his contact person. We would have spoken with him directly but we've been unable to get ahold of him. He came in a few times during this timeframe to donate."

"Uh, yeah, about that. You haven't been able to reach him because Noah passed. He's-he's gone."

"Oh, Grace, I'm so sorry for your loss. I can only image. He was always a sweet guy when he came in. I'll never forget him. He was tall, dark, and very handsome. Had the smile to make any woman fall at his knees."

Her comment brings me to laughter, helping me to suppress the tears that were mounting.

"How much of his specimen do you have? Has any of it been used? Oh, God, has anyone else used the sperm? Does he have other children out in the world?"

"Oh, no! Goodness, no! He donated the sperm in exchange for money it seems. Because the sperm was never used, we contacted him a few years back, maybe 2014 or 2015 according to his file, and he requested we keep it on file. We asked him for a contact person and he said Grace Middleton. None of the sperm has been used, per his request."

I exhale deeply, as her words provide me with some comfort. I've been through enough; I don't think I could handle knowing another woman has Noah's child.

"So, we have a couple of forms here that you can, depending on what route you want to take. Disposal paperwork is here, transferring paperwork here, or you can sign this form here and use the specimen yourself. If you need further explanation on anything, that's what I'm here for."

The receptionist places her hand on each stack as she speaks. My eyes shift back and forth between the paperwork. I never thought I'd have to make this type of decision, ever. I already have Noah's legacy. We have our baby. Should I really be thinking about having another?

"I can see you'll need some time. Take as much as you need, and I'll come back and check on you."

The receptionist retreats and leaves me alone to decide.

***

"Hey sweetheart, we're glad to hear from you. I've been calling you for hours. Are you ok?"

"I'm fine, Mom. Thanks for keeping Noah. I'm about to come over and pick him up now."

"Are you sure? Naomi said she was about to come over there anyway. She was going to bring him home, that was why I was calling you. You sure everything is ok? You said you had to run a couple of errands."

"I did, and everything is fine. Tell Naomi to stay put, I'm coming over."

The hesitance in my mother's voice is apparent, but she'll be fine, especially when she hears what I need to tell her. I haven't been able to catch up with anyone in quite some time. Shortly after Noah Junior's birthday, I got a major response to a new website I designed, and I've been busy with that, all while trying to make my deadlines, which isn't always easy with a small child and doctor's visits every two weeks. It's been a month, and I'm just now able to breathe again.

In no time, I arrive at my parent's place.

"Hi sweetheart, I saw you pulling up so I wanted to go ahead and open the door."

"Thanks Dad." I kiss him on the cheek and squeeze past with a bag in my hand.

"Did you come bearing gifts?" Naomi asks, her eyebrows rise inquisitively.

"I did. Where's Noah?" I look around and notice Mom and Noah are both missing.

"He's in the back. Your mother was laying him down just a moment ago," Dad answers and I slip around the edge of the couch and take a seat.

"Dad, can you get us four wine glasses please?"

Dad's eyes are filled with curiosity as I reach down into the bag I brought in and pull out a bottle of Clos Des Papes Magnum that Noah and I were given at our wedding reception. I've been saving it all this time, waiting for a good time to open the bottle. Noah and I promised one another we'd open it for our tenth-year anniversary, but we never made it to that point.

Us popping the bottle open today still holds importance though.

Dad leaves the room and goes into the kitchen. Naomi saunters over to me, sliding in like she knows something.

"So…what are we celebrating? I've seen that bottle and I know it's for special occasions only, so what is the special occasion?" Naomi clasps her hands together, wiggling around in excitement.

"Just wait til' Mom comes out and then I'll tell everybody."

Mom shows.

"I tried to keep him up for you, but he was fading. Is that *the* Clos Des Papes Magnum? Oh goodness, what's going on?" Mom asks, directing her attention to the bottle. Dad reemerges from the kitchen with the glasses I asked for.

He places the glasses on the coffee table and Mom sits at the other end of the couch. Dad's favorite chair is next to me, so he pops into his recliner and gets comfortable. I woke to open the bottle and pour of some wine for everyone to enjoy. I pass each glass around, wanting them to have their glasses in hand before I say anything further.

"So, there are a few things I want to share with everybody, but I don't want anyone to start freaking out." I wait a minute to allow everyone a chance to get their faces together. Mom looks like she's ready to break down crying, and she doesn't even know what's going on yet. Dad seems to be holding it together, but that's something he's always done. Naomi's face is calm, but she can't stop twiddling her fingers. I know she'll be the one to lose it all before I get to the end.

"So, for the last month and a half, I've continued going to the doctor every two weeks. I've been getting checkups, eating better, and just trying to stay the course I think God has put me on. A month ago, I told you guys that I was in remission…"

Mom's stomach visibly turns. She has one hand on her belly, and my father reaches out for my hand.

"Well, I'm no longer in remission."

Naomi squeezes my hand, scooting closer to me, and then I continue. "I'm no longer in remission because I'm cancer free!" I jump up off the couch, bouncing left to right. Picking up my glass, I swish it around and tilt it back, leaving not a speck of wine behind.

"Oh, my goodness! Oh, my goodness!" Mom jumps around. Naomi wraps her arms around my neck, and Mom joins in behind her. Dad joins in too, and now we're all standing here huddled together as the family we are.

"That's not it," I say almost suffocating under my family's love.

"There's more? Your cancer being cured is a miracle honey! What did they say? I'm a proud mother."

Now I'm the one who has to keep from crying. My mother looks like she's on the verge of a positive emotional breakdown.

"They say it was like nothing they'd ever seen. The cancer cells are completely gone. It was almost like I never even had it!" I lean over the table and pour myself another glass. Naomi follows suit and takes a swig of hers.

"My, my, my. This is great news Grace. I'd like to make a toast."

"Well, before you do that, hold on Dad. I gotta tell y'all the other part."

Everyone starts to sit down, but I interrupt, "But please, have a drink. Dad, you can make a toast another time."

We all laugh and get comfortable again.

"So, on Noah's birthday, I received a phone call from Stanton Fertility Cryobank. They mentioned something about closing out an old account Noah had. So, they schedule me an appointment and I went. Come to find out, Noah donated sperm some years back and left my name as a contact. It's crazy because during the time he donated to the cryobank we weren't in contact with one another. After high school, we didn't see one another again until the class reunion. He donated and left my name, my maiden name, there as a point of contact long before we reunited and married.

Naomi looks like she's going to burst at the seams. I can almost feel what she's feeling. Nobody moves. Even their faces are still.

"Oh my God, are you saying you're pregnant?!" Mom shouts, and I burst into laughter.

"No. I'm telling you that we have the opportunity. Well, I have the opportunity if I ever see fit to have another child by my husband."

The sound of everyone gasping is overwhelming, but they all have the same expression I do—a smile. Having NJ was the best thing I could have ever done, and if I use this sperm, he won't have to be alone.

"Thank you, Jesus! Thank you, Lord! My daughter is gonna be just fine! Amen!" Mom stands and shouts. She comes right to me, embracing me. Just as before, we all end up huddled together in hug formation.

"I love you, Grace," Naomi speaks through her tears.

"I love you, too. I love each of you. You know, this is simply confirmation to me from God. I'm covered and I always have been, even though there were times I didn't see what was happening."

I have encountered so many miracles. God's favor never left me, even when I thought he didn't have me. I'm so thankful for everything God has given me. He continues to bless me, even when I thought He'd given up on me. He was always right there.

EPILOGUE

Two years later

"Come on, baby, let's go see Daddy." I lean down to grab NJ's hand as we get out of the car. It's Noah's birthday. I thought it would be fitting to bring NJ to the cemetery to visit his father. It's been quite some time since our last visit.

We cross the street and aim for the tree that rests on the back of the property. We buried him in this location, so I would always have a marker for where he was. Though looking back now, I could never forget where he is, even in my worst state of being, it isn't something that's easily forgotten.

Reaching his headstone, I position myself down onto my knees. This seems to be more comfortable than standing. Without direction, NJ nestles down quietly beside me. I take his small hand in mine and use my other hand to run my fingertips over the letting on Noah's headstone.

"Hi, handsome. I haven't been here in a while, but it's your birthday, and I wanted us to spend some time with you and catch you up to speed." I clear my throat and fight the tears so that I may continue to speak without interruption.

"My business has really taken off, and with it, my time has been little to none. but I'm thankful. This was the best decision I could have made for NJ and myself. It's given me more freedom to raise our rambunctious toddler."

I giggle a bit and kiss N.J. on his chubby cheek. Preparing to speak again, a cold chill moves over my skin as a gust of wind brushes against me. The familiarity in scent and feeling lets me know it's my husband. Before I look up to confirm, NJ stands straight up. Balancing himself, he takes a few steps away from me. Reaching out to him, I'm forced to look up where I see NJ standing beside Noah, his little hand in the air, holding on so lovingly to his father's hand.

Shock consumes me. I wasn't aware that NJ could ever see his father. I thought I was the only one.

Noah leans down and kisses NJ on the forehead, and together, they come back to me, getting in the same position I'm in on the ground. Noah carries a smile on his face, but it looks like more of a smirk. I can't help but to smile as he comes closer to me and places his hand on my growing stomach.

"I couldn't help myself. I figured, we did so good with the first one, why not have another?" I explain, looking down at his hand that's now caressing the surface of my stomach. "I'm eight months, nearly due. There have been no complications and no sign of my cancer returning. I'm completely healthy and so is our baby."

The news causes Noah's body to adopt this glow that's

unexplainable around his aura. He looks to be happy, peaceful, and he's dressed differently than he was when I was sick. He has on a tailored suit; the fit he wore when we wed.

"You're dressed awfully nice for a visit," I say, as NJ climbs back up into my lap.

"I wanted it to be romantic. Sue me," Noah says, shrugging his shoulder, laughing, but I can tell he has more to say. I'm not struggling to get to my feet until Noah reaches out and takes my hand, pulling me up the rest of the way.

"Thank you," I say, dusting off my palms.

It's silent between us for a moment. He's searching for the right words to say, and I'm ready to hear them, I think.

"I'm proud of you, you know. I'm glad you sold the town-house and made the lake house your home permanently."

That's something I have had a hard time in the past with, but when it came down to it, I spent so much more time in the lake house when I was struggling, it gave me peace and made me feel free. Holding onto the townhouse was a last-ditch effort to hold onto some normalcy, and my life is anything but.

"It was time to let it go. I lived a wonderful life there, but that house...I could never go back. Not where you took your last breath. It wouldn't be the same."

"I know, that's why I'm glad you didn't force yourself to keep it. I'm sorry I haven't been around as often, as much as I used to."

I hear the defeat in his voice, the disappointment.

"No, don't apologize. I get it. You were there most when I needed you, and that's more than I can ever say or be grateful for. You were my rock, for better or worse, in this lifetime, and

I have faith our souls will meet in the next. You had our backs more than you even know."

My words come out as choking thoughts telling Noah the truth behind what I know. He came to save me. Without him, I wouldn't have made it. I would have constantly ignored the signs of my sickness, pushed away my parents and Naomi. I probably would have died out there all alone, not knowing our child was growing inside me or that cancer was progressively eating away at my body. I've seen God's power; his grace and his mercy. I know Noah is a gift from God, and now I have to return him.

Noah nods, and our bodies become drawn together like a moth to a flame. His lips slowly collide into mine. The kiss is so passionate, it feels as if we're kissing for the first time again. The kiss is so sweet, so refreshing, I know it will last a lifetime.

As Noah wraps his arms around me, NJ comes between us, kissing my belly, talking to his little sister. This is something he often does and enjoys spending as much time as he can with my belly.

"I love you, both of you, and I will watch over you until the end of time. Nothing will keep me from the three of you. Take care of yourself Grace, love yourself first and everything else will come into alignment," Noah confesses as his body begins to fade. He looks to NJ and my belly one last time, "I love you, my legacies."

Noah releases his embrace and takes a step back. NJ and I watch as Noah's body fades and dissolves into the ground and into his grave.

Careful not to linger and get in my feelings, I tug at NJ's arm and trek back toward the car. Waiting to cross the street, tears cascade down my cheeks onto my blouse. I'm not disappointed, I just miss my husband. I will forever miss the love we shared, but I'm thankful for it, thankful 5for your reunion. It brought us a beautiful son, and an unborn child that's sure to be an exact replica of Noah and NJ. I've seen it in a dream already.

At the vehicle, I fasten NJ into his seat and before closing the door I glance back over my shoulder once more to get a look at the gravesite.

"Bye Daddy, bye!" N.J. shouts over me, looking at his father's headstone.

I smile and close the door, standing there for a moment longer. The wind wraps around me like a warm blanket. I embrace it. I know Noah will always be with me, even if I can't see him. I can feel his presence in everything I do. He'll live on through his children, who will grow up to know the beauty of the man that was their father, that he was a good man, a loving husband, and a faithful protector and provider. I don't know if Noah or God know but having him return truly saved my life. God and Noah saved Grace Richardson. They…saved…me.

"I love you," I whisper to the wind, one last time before getting into the car. Now we head home, back to the lake house.

The End

Hey There!

Thank you for your support on my literary journey. I hope your reading experience was a pleasant one. Please leave a review on Goodreads and Amazon. Please feel free to connect with me to stay current on upcoming releases and reader specific exclusives.

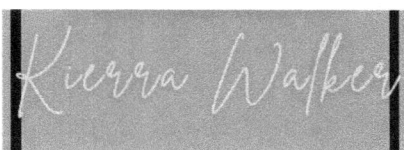

AUTHOR KIERRA WALKER

Author Kierra Walker is an Arkansas native, her roots embedded in the southeast region of the state.

Walker has garnered much acclaim for her bestselling titles *Saving Grace* and *Inmate #02071987* and has successfully published several other bestselling titles.

Kierra's eclectic, compassionate, and charismatic nature serves as the foundational layer to each storyline she pens.

Join Kierra Walker as she grants readers access to the innermost portions of her mind through heartfelt classics with captivating narratives, hints of drama, and comedic flair.

KIERRA WALKER'S CATALOG

Inmate #02071987
Hell Hath No Fury: Fool Me Once
Boy Meets Girl
The Rebound

CONNECT WITH KIERRA WALKER

Join my readers group on Facebook for discussions, sneak peeks, exclusive content, and access to other great authors. Reader's Paradise

Scan the image below with your phone's camera to connect with authorkierrawalker.com.